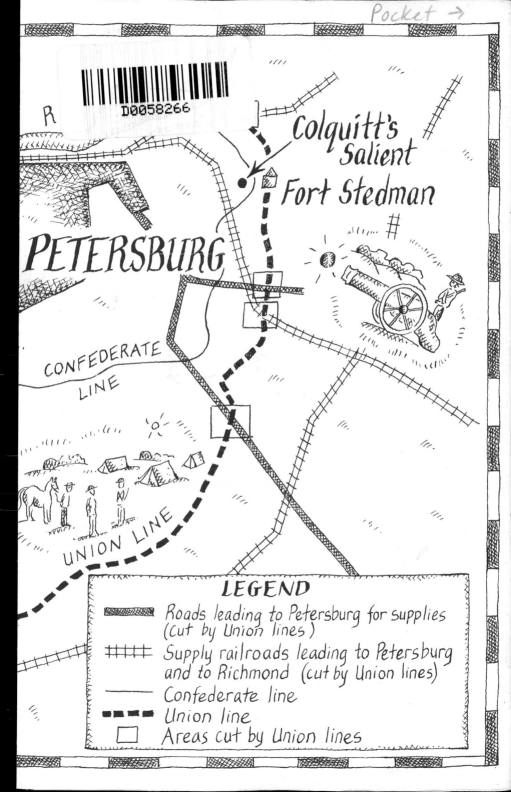

Pocket →

R

D0058266

Colquitt's
Salient

Fort Stedman

PETERSBURG

CONFEDERATE
LINE

UNION LINE

LEGEND

Roads leading to Petersburg for supplies
(cut by Union lines)

Supply railroads leading to Petersburg
and to Richmond (cut by Union lines)

Confederate line

Union line

Areas cut by Union lines

3 1432 00097 7221

YA   Alphin, Elaine Marie

                 Ghost soldier

11/02

DISCARD

Boulder City Library
701 Adams Boulevard
Boulder City, NV 89005

GHOST SOLDIER

ELAINE MARIE ALPHIN

Boulder City Library
701 Adams Boulevard
Boulder City, NV 89005
DISCARD
SEP ···· 2002

Henry Holt and Company
New York

Henry Holt and Company, LLC
Publishers since 1866
115 West 18th Street
New York, New York 10011

Henry Holt is a registered trademark
of Henry Holt and Company, LLC

Copyright © 2001 by Elaine Marie Alphin
Map copyright © 2001 by Jennifer Thermes
All rights reserved.
Distributed in Canada by H. B. Fenn and Company Ltd.

Library of Congress Cataloging-in-Publication Data
Alphin, Elaine Marie.
Ghost soldier / Elaine Marie Alphin.
p.   cm.
Summary: Alexander, in North Carolina while his father decides whether to remarry and
move there, meets the ghost of a Confederate soldier and helps him look for his family.
[1. Ghosts—Fiction.   2. North Carolina—History—Civil War, 1861–1865—Fiction.
3. Brothers and sisters—Fiction.   4. Fathers and sons—Fiction.   5. Durham (N.C.)—
Fiction.   6. United States—History—Civil War, 1861–1865—Fiction.]   I. Title.
PZ7.A4625 Gj   2001   [Fic]—dc21   00-54400
ISBN 0-8050-6158-4
First Edition—2001 / Design by David Caplan
Printed in the United States of America on acid-free paper. ∞

1   3   5   7   9   10   8   6   4   2

For Art,
who continues
to stand fast
against great odds

Contents

GHOST
SOLDIER

Chapter One

WINDOW
THROUGH TIME

"Need a hand with your bag?" Dad asked over his shoulder.

"No." I looked at the wreck of a house in front of us as he started down the driveway to Mrs. Hambrick's home.

"Come on, Alexander. You'll see—this spring break is going to be special—for both of us."

For him, maybe. I slung my backpack over my shoulder, but I didn't pick up my duffel bag. "What if Mom comes back and finds our house empty? She'll never know to look for us down here in North Carolina."

Dad's knuckles whitened on the handle of his suitcase. He was already puffing a little from his own suitcase and computer bag—he doesn't work out except when he runs with me, so he's kind of overweight. "It's been over three years," he said, not turning back to me.

Three years, two months, and twenty-three days, I thought to myself. She left on New Year's Day, just before I turned ten.

Dad finished, "I've told you before—she's not coming back."

He keeps saying that, but I don't believe it. My dad's okay—he writes computer software for a living. That makes the other kids back home in Indiana think I'm the luckiest guy in the world, because our house is wired with the latest computer stuff. I agree it's great to mess around with new systems and know all the Easter Egg secret programs and jokes the programmers hide in their software. But Dad has lived with computers so long he expects everything to work out logically, like programming code. Mom isn't anything like computer code. She's like the music she plays on her recorder and like the flowers she grows—one minute bubbling over with happiness, then sad and droopy the next. I was sure she'd just appear one day, the way she'd left, so I'd tried to keep everything perfect for her.

I picked up the duffel and glared at Mrs. Hambrick's overgrown yard—the sight of this disaster made me feel even worse about getting dragged here. The ivy and Virginia creeper grew thick, choking any flowers that even thought about pushing up through them. Shrill crickets hid in the undergrowth, but the grass was really sparse—only a few limp blades trying to grow in the shadows of oaks and maples that hadn't been pruned in what seemed like forever. I hadn't let our yard grow wild like that. Our bulbs had already come up.

"This place is falling apart," I muttered.

But Dad just said, "Look at these quiet streets—it's a great place to run." He grinned. "I bet you'll get a ribbon at your next meet."

I remembered him cheering the last time I competed. It was embarrassing and great at the same time. The only thing that would have been better was if Mom had been there, too. And if I'd placed, of course.

But I wasn't going to let him change the subject, no matter how important track was to me. "I mean it—look at the bricks, with all those white smears. How hard can it be to keep two stories' worth of bricks red? And look at those overgrown trees—"

"The Hambricks bought the place to fix it up," Dad said. "The walls used to be whitewashed—that's why the bricks look funny. They'd barely stripped the whitewash when the accident happened."

I didn't answer. I just stared at the dingy white louvered doors, half hidden behind once-white columns whose paint was now cracked and peeling. Wind chimes hung from the front porch, jangling shrill musical notes and flashing unexpectedly when a ray of sunshine squeezed through the trees and hit them. Was I supposed to say I was sorry Mr. Hambrick died? I was. He'd been killed in a car accident. Some driver who wasn't paying attention ran a red light and hit him. Sure I was sorry it happened. If he were still alive, we wouldn't be here visiting Mrs. Hambrick and her kids.

Before Dad could say anything else, one of the louvered doors creaked open, rattling the wind chimes, and Mrs. Hambrick came out. Her short blond hair stuck up in every direction like she'd forgotten to comb it.

"Bill!" Mrs. Hambrick smiled at my dad as if she'd just gotten the most terrific present. "Even after your last e-mail, I could hardly believe you were really on your way!"

"Hi, Paige," he said, his voice so low I could barely hear him.

Then she tore her eyes away and looked at me. "Alexander—I was delighted when I got your father's e-mail saying that you'd decided to come. Carleton and Nicole are excited to meet you!"

Her voice was the same soft Southern drawl I remembered from meeting her in Indianapolis. I hadn't bothered to listen to it then, but now that soft heavy accent threatened to smother me. I couldn't think of anything to say, so I kept my mouth shut. But it didn't matter. She wasn't paying attention to me. She was smiling at Dad, and he was smiling back at her. They looked kind of weird together—Dad with his balding head and what rust-colored hair he did have pulled back in a ponytail, and her with her hair standing up all over the place. Dad's stocky and she's skinny, and both of them were wearing faded jeans and sweatshirts. That's what Dad wears all the time, but he doesn't go to an office or anything—he just writes his software programs at home and sends them in by FedEx, so nobody sees him. Anyway, all computer gurus dress that way. It's like a uniform. But Mrs. Hambrick is some kind of professor at Duke University—you'd think she'd look, well, more dignified.

The front door banged behind them, setting the wind chimes ringing again, and a little kid, who looked about seven, with curly brown hair and a big grin ran down the dirt path toward us, jumping over the roots that stuck up in his way. It had to be Carleton.

"Hi! You're Alex, aren't you?" he cried, leaning back to look up at me. I wasn't that tall yet—just about Dad's height, but I had a lean runner's build. I guess I looked tall to Carleton. "You get to share my room! You even get to sleep on my dinosaur sheets—they're my favorite! Mom said you like history. Do you like dinosaur history, or only people history?"

Did this kid ever run down? And why did I have to share a room with him? I looked at my dad, who wouldn't meet my eyes.

"Well, do you?" Carleton insisted.

"People history, I guess," I said, thinking about the history stories Mom used to tell me. His smile kind of shrunk away, so I added, "Dinosaur history, too."

He lit up again. "Stegosaurus is my favorite," he told me.

Dad still hadn't said anything, but he was smiling at Carleton, and I suddenly wished I hadn't said anything good about dinosaur history.

"It's just for the week, Alexander," Mrs. Hambrick said quickly. "Carleton is so excited at the idea of sharing with you. We have another room upstairs, but it doesn't have furniture yet."

"Are you Mr. Raskin?" the kid asked, turning to my dad. "Are you going to be my new father?"

Mrs. Hambrick's neck flushed bright red, and my dad practically dropped his suitcase. Even the crickets stopped chirping. I felt like saying, No. Never. He's *my* father. And I *hate* dinosaurs.

But I kept my mouth shut. What was the point? Dad never listened to me anymore. He'd even made me go to a counselor at school for a while.

I dropped my duffel bag, stepped over the tree roots, and went around Carleton, who just stood there grinning happily. It didn't matter anyway. Dad wasn't going to marry Mrs. Hambrick. I was going to wait for Mom to come home, no matter what—like the family in this story she told me. Mom always told me history stories at bedtime instead of fairy tales. She really liked to tell the one about Odysseus, who went off to war and took ten years to get back home. His wife and son vowed to wait for him. Other men wanted to marry Odysseus' wife, but she told them she couldn't say yes to any of them until she finished weaving a special cloth. She spent all day weaving and all night ripping out what she'd stitched. That way she'd never finish, so she and her son would be waiting for Odysseus when he came home.

I hadn't figured out a way to make Dad take up weaving in order to chase away women like Mrs. Hambrick, though. I'd have to work on that. I just kept telling myself everything would be okay in the end. Odysseus came home, and Mom would come home, too. And Dad and I would be waiting.

I followed the shadowy path as it climbed through damp, spongy soil and undergrowth. There had to be some quiet place where I could be alone. I turned the corner around the far end of the house, and suddenly a voice came down from right above me. "So—was the brat right? Is your father going to marry my mother?"

My heart jumped but I looked up, trying to keep my cool. A porch was nestled in an L-shaped cut in the house, and a girl sat there on a wooden swing, staring at me with a half smile. Not a friendly smile. I hoped she hadn't seen any reaction—she was probably trying to spook me.

"Nicole?" I guessed. I found myself fiddling nervously with the loose ends of the braided leather lariat I'd tied onto my left wrist before we left. Mom had made it. I used to wear it all the time, but I hadn't worn it much the last year or so. I'd made up my mind to wear it every day on this trip, though.

"And you're Alex," she told me, like I was an idiot or something. She fiddled with the ends of her short blond hair. "We've seen the photos, you know."

"It's Alexander," I said. I knew about the photos. Mrs. Hambrick had taken pictures while we went sightseeing in Indianapolis last fall, when she came for a computer conference. Dad met her that summer at some computer exposition.

Dad invited me to the Indianapolis conference but didn't give me any grief when I said I didn't want to go. He dragged me along to dinner on Saturday night, though, to meet Mrs. Hambrick. Then he made plans for all of us to spend Sunday together in the city before she flew back home. He'd actually worn a sports jacket and a tie to dinner, even though he pulled the tie loose before we got to the restaurant and had it practically off before the food came. She'd shown us pictures of her kids, but I hadn't paid attention. I never thought I'd meet them.

"Okay, Al-ex-an-der," Nicole said, dragging out the syllables. "So—is Carleton right about our parents? Mom's been hogging the phone lines Instant Messaging your father just about every night."

I stared back at her, not letting her see my surprise. Now and then Dad had mentioned something Mrs. Hambrick had told him, but I figured they just e-mailed once in a while. "What do you think?"

Nicole shrugged. "I don't care what they do. A couple more years of high school, then I'm out of here—and you can bet I won't be going to college at Duke! I'm going someplace far away, where nobody's ever heard of my mother or her probability research. If she marries your father, so what?"

Yeah, right. She wouldn't go so far away if it didn't matter to her. But she obviously didn't want to admit it. I steered clear of some poison ivy and climbed up the wooden steps to the porch. "You really should cut back some of those trees,"

I said, sitting on the top step. I thought I could smell sweet honeysuckle in the air, and I liked it. And since there weren't any clanging wind chimes back here, it was kind of peaceful. "I mean—shade is okay for some plants, but most flowers won't grow without sunlight."

"What's it to you?" Nicole said. She was playing with her hair again. "Gardening is for girls, anyway."

"Yeah?" I snapped. "Well, the best gardeners—the ones who plan out mazes and stuff like that—are men. And you *girls* have sure done a rotten job with *this* garden!"

A glass door slid open behind us. "I see you two have met," said Mrs. Hambrick. She sounded kind of nervous.

Nicole jumped off the swing, setting the chains jangling as loudly as the wind chimes. "Moth-errr!" she snarled.

She made the word sound like an insult, but my eyes suddenly blurred. It had been such a long time since I'd called anyone that.

Nicole slipped past her mother into the house.

Mrs. Hambrick stood there as if she wanted to say something. I just stared at the yard and tried not to think about her. I thought I saw some blackberry brambles in the tangle of vines. If they were cut back, they might actually grow some berries.

Finally Mrs. Hambrick said, "I've fixed a welcome supper for you and your father, Alexander. Not so fancy as the meal at that restaurant y'all took me out to, of course, but I hope you'll like it. Would you like to put your things in Carleton's room and clean up, then come back down? It's upstairs, the second door on the left—the one with all the dinosaurs."

I could think of plenty of reasons why I didn't want to leave my stuff in Carleton's room and come down to supper. But I just said thanks and crossed the living room to the stairs. Every flat surface in the room was crowded with crystal sculptures—stars and mountains and leaping animals—all cut like jewels. I felt like I was walking through the broken heart of a geode. I grabbed my duffel by the foyer and hurried up the stairs. From the music blaring behind a closed door, I guessed Nicole's room was at the far end of the hall.

I had no trouble recognizing Carleton's room. The kid hadn't just given me his dinosaur sheets—he'd put a weird green stuffed dragon on top of the bed. I guess it was supposed to be a stegosaurus. A zooful of animals sat on the other bed, some of them threadbare and squashed out of shape. The stegosaurus looked pretty good in comparison. Both beds were covered with quilts decorated with brightly colored dancing dinosaurs. There was even a dinosaur wind chime. I couldn't help smiling a little as I washed up for supper.

The sailboat wind chimes in the bathroom window clinked softly in the breeze. I stared at myself in the streaky mirror and saw my mother's black eyes under my father's russet hair, and my smile disappeared. Why hadn't Dad said anything when Carleton asked him about being his new father? And why wasn't I sharing a room with *him*, instead of with a little kid and a bunch of dinosaurs?

Dad was waiting for me at the bottom of the stairs and beckoned me down a hall, past the kitchen into a room near the garage. It must have been Mrs. Hambrick's office, since there was a computer on a desk. Dad's PowerBook laptop was set up beside her monitor. He'd really made himself at home—he'd even brought his little Space Warrior model and set him out on the desk.

Computer programmers put in these secret programs you can find if you hit the right combination of keys. Of all the ones Dad's written, his favorite is this Space Warrior he drew that erases whatever's on the screen. When you hit the right keys, the Space Warrior runs out and fires his ray gun at the place you want to erase until he's made it all disappear—sound effects and everything. Dad calls him the Defender of the Galaxy. He even found a metal gaming figure that looked like his drawing at the hobby store, and fixed him up with a little ray gun and painted him like the Space Warrior.

A sofa folded out into a bed, and Dad's open suitcase took up most of the floor space that was left. I felt a little better about rooming with Carleton. There sure wasn't room for me down here. More wind chimes hung in the window. Their clanging was getting on my nerves.

11

Dad sat on the bed and looked at me. "Alexander, I need your help this week. We've got to work together—be a team."

I picked up the Space Warrior and turned it over in my hand. Dad made a big deal out of teamwork. That was okay with me. I knew how important teamwork was from track. I even had ninth graders like Gary Shaw cheering me when I ran. But that was different.

"Look," Dad said. "I'm sorry you're sharing with Carleton. It's only for spring break. Later—"

"Later I'll be home," I told him, even though it was only Thursday night and it seemed a long time until the end of spring break. "So it doesn't matter."

He reached out and touched my arm. "Alexander, we talked about this. I want to marry Paige—I want you to get to know her."

Clenching the Space Warrior, I thought, We all want things we don't get. When I didn't answer, Dad sighed. "Just be polite and give her a chance. Okay?"

He didn't have to worry. Nicole was rude enough at supper for both of us. She slumped in her seat, gave long, exaggerated sighs when her mother asked her to pass a dish, made faces at the food, and answered in grunts. She'd said more to me on the porch than she said during the entire meal. Carleton wouldn't shut up, though, distracting the grown-ups. So nobody paid any attention to me, which was fine. I just enjoyed the food.

I ate my way through a spinach salad, which tasted a lot better than it sounded, and pork chops glazed with pieces of some sort of tart fruit. They looked weird, but tasted good. Dad wasn't much of a cook, so this was a treat. I just kept my mouth full so I didn't have to talk much, and passed dishes when I was asked. It was easy enough to fade into the background. *Yes, ma'am, it's really good. Sure, a little more, thanks. The corn muffins are good. I'll have a piece of blackberry pie.* That bramble must have some berries on it after all.

Dad smiled at me when we got up from the table. Nicole flounced off to her room, probably to listen to CDs again, and Carleton was yawning, so I went upstairs and dug a T-shirt out of my duffel to sleep in, so that I wouldn't wake him later. Then I took my recorder case and some music books out of my backpack and went down to the porch. Dad and Mrs. Hambrick were talking in low voices in the living room, and I heard Dad laugh, but I didn't want to listen to them. I just wanted to make some music.

Mom plays the recorder. I'd taught myself on a little soprano recorder as soon as I learned how to read the sheet music. It wasn't hard. Other kids played the recorder in music class, but I never played with them. It was just for Mom and me, not for school. Now I had an alto recorder—it was bigger, and it had a mellow tone I liked. Mom would be thrilled I'd taught myself, and we could play duets. I took the pieces out of their case, put the recorder together, and blew a few notes softly. The tangled branches of the overgrown trees clacked like percussion, and my recorder notes blended in with them.

Enough light came through the living room window for me to read the music easily, and I warmed up with some folk tunes I nearly knew by heart. Then I practiced some harder songs, working on the fingering until I got the notes right. The rustling of the branches faded after a while, and all I heard was the recorder, crystal clear on the cold air. It felt colder at night here than it did in Indiana, which surprised me. The shadows grew darker, and a hazy mist was rising. I stretched my fingers and reached for the recorder's cleaning rod. Then I stopped.

Suddenly the chill air smelled tangy, like those pork chops at supper—almost like someone had cut open a ripe orange and spurted the juice all over the porch. I felt a thrill go through me as time seemed to stand still in the tangled yard. It was happening again, after so long.

I held my breath as I heard faint clopping, and a mixture of creaking and jangling came from the far side of the yard, like someone riding a horse. Then I heard the heavy tramp of marching feet, boots scraping on stones or thudding on the ground. The light from the living room disappeared, and I squinted through the tree trunks choked by mist in the moonlight to make out a group of men wearing broad-brimmed hats.

When one of them turned to say something to another, I couldn't hear the words. But the mist thinned for a moment, and I could see the two of them plainly, down to the lines in the taller man's face, above his beard. He looked dirty, and so tired that he stumbled as he walked. Moonlight glinted gold near his throat—a shiny coat button. The face that looked up to his was younger and just as grubby, though the second soldier didn't have a beard. His eyes were large and black, like deep wells. Then the moonlight shimmered silver beside the two faces, and I saw that each man was holding a gun up to his shoulder. The others carried some sort of rifles, too.

I stood up unsteadily, amazed and delighted, and scared I'd miss something. Then the taller man turned away, and the mist thickened to hide his companion. I gripped the cold porch railing in one hand and my recorder in the other and strained to see past the trees again. But clouds had covered the moon, and the marching men disappeared into shadow. I realized I was sweating—now the night felt warmer again and almost stuffy. The lights had come back on in the living room, and my shadow spilled down the porch steps. When I sniffed the air, I could smell that hint of early honeysuckle, but the tang of oranges had vanished with the soldiers.

I felt breathless and drained—and also a little sad, as if I'd been part of something and then it had gone and left me. But I'd seen them again—ghosts. When Mom came back, I could tell her about the soldiers in the mist.

Chapter Two

WHO YOUR FAMILY WAS

The next morning I got up early, pulled on running sweats, and headed out of the house. Dad was right—the quiet streets around the university were perfect for running, with the new leaves uncurling on the bushes and trees around me. But the country roads back home were perfect, too.

Dad should have made that early morning run with me, but he was still asleep when I left Carleton tangled in his sheets. I didn't care—I'd run without Dad plenty of times. Sometimes I liked it better alone. I could zone out, the way I did on cross-country runs for track. My legs kept the pace going, but the world got hot and dark and my mind loosened up, and I remembered the first time I'd seen ghosts.

I was only five. The smell of oranges woke me, and I couldn't go back to sleep because it was so cold. I got up and looked outside and saw Indians—not like the Native American kids I knew from school, but barefoot Indians with threadbare blankets draped over their shoulders.

The next day, Mom told me I'd found a window through time, but that night the scene had seemed like it was happening right then. They were standing in a line. When each Indian got to the front of the line, he gave something to a man. I couldn't see it clearly, but I knew it was a dollar, which must have been a lot of money back then. They got a needle for their dollar—one needle! I could hear the man telling them, "These are the last needles in the world. The man who made them is dead."

Mom told me that what I had seen had really happened—a white settler cheated some Native Americans in Indiana by selling needles for a dollar. She told me I was special. But then, why had she left me? People who love you don't just walk away from you forever. I remembered her getting mad at me for trying to help her in the garden; I had pulled up some of the tiny seedlings, thinking they were weeds. She had been so disappointed in me. I shut out the thought and ran until the bushes lining the road and the asphalt under my running shoes seemed to disappear, and I saw only the ghosts from the night before.

Mrs. Hambrick was taking Dad to meet some of her "good friends" at the university that afternoon, and she wanted me to come along, as well. I was torn. The last thing I wanted to do was sit in some college dining hall listening to a bunch of boring adults. But I didn't want to leave Dad alone with Mrs. Hambrick and those good friends of hers, either.

In the end, it didn't matter what I wanted. Dad said I had to come with them. I told him I only had T-shirts and an old Apple computer sweatshirt with holes in the sleeves, unless he wanted me to wear my running sweats—not exactly the right clothes for a fancy faculty club.

But Dad said the place wasn't that fancy. He dug through my duffel bag and pulled out a plaid flannel shirt I'd brought to wear over the T-shirts, and said I'd look okay if I wore that, all buttoned up.

"Why do I have to get dressed up like this?" I asked him. "I look like a geek!" Even dumber than you do in your jacket, with loose hairs pulling out of your ponytail, I thought, but I didn't say it out loud.

"Trust me," Dad said, grinning, "I've seen plenty of geeks, and you don't look anything like one." Then his round face got serious. "Do it for me, Alexander, okay? Paige is important to me. I've told you that. And these are people we'll see a lot of when we move here."

"I live in Indiana," I told him. "Not here."

Dad sat down on Carleton's bed and fidgeted with a stuffed tyrannosaurus. "I know you wish things were different, Alexander, but your mother's not coming back."

"She will," I said, even if he didn't want to hear it. I twisted the leather lariat as if it was a tether binding her to me.

"Alexander," Dad said, and his voice sounded muffled, as if he were trying not to cry. Maybe he did hope Mom would come back, but he just couldn't quite believe it. Maybe it's harder to believe in someone when you're grown up. Then he looked at me and said, "Your mother left us, and I divorced her."

So what? Mom didn't show up in court, so maybe she didn't know she was divorced. If you can undo a marriage, can't you undo a divorce? "You'll see," I said calmly, staring him right in the eye. "She'll be back."

"You're like a program stuck in an endless loop!" He sounded exasperated, but he was the one who looked away. "Please, Alexander—just give Paige a chance, for me? You'll like her—if you just let yourself. She knows you like history, so she's set up this trip to a Civil War battlefield on Saturday. I want you to enjoy it."

But I didn't want to like her. "Why does she think I like history?" I asked, wondering what else she thought she knew about me.

Dad blinked, surprised. "I told her you did. I mean— you've got all those books about the Trojan War and those posters of Greece up on your walls . . ." His voice trailed off.

He really didn't understand. Maybe he didn't remember Mom's stories. But all I said was, "Mom's stories about the Trojan War aren't the same as the Civil War, Dad. I'm not interested."

He stood up suddenly and dropped the toy dinosaur on Carleton's bed. "Well, act interested this weekend." And he strode out of the room.

I still felt like a geek when we got to the Great Hall, but the other two professors didn't seem to mind how either Dad or I looked. They talked about computers and teaching and asked questions about Indiana, then told Dad how much he was going to like North Carolina.

I just sat there not paying much attention to them, glad I could get something ordinary like a cheeseburger.

"So you like history, Alexander?" Dr. Seagraves asked, her black eyes curious.

I mumbled, "Sure, I guess—some history, anyway."

"Well, Alexander is certainly the name for a history lover," she said, smiling as she speared a lettuce leaf. "Alexander the Great, you know."

I remembered that Mrs. Hambrick said Dr. Seagraves taught history. I thought about telling her my mom loved history—she named me for Alexander the Great. But I felt funny talking about Mom in this place. So I just nodded and stuffed a french fry in my mouth.

"Alexander plays the recorder," Mrs. Hambrick said. "Another tie with history."

Dr. Seagraves looked at me as if I'd just done something very interesting. "That *is* quite an historic instrument. Does your music teacher have you play medieval rondos and ballads in class?"

I swallowed the french fry, wondering what to answer. Everybody was looking at me. I finally said, "Well, I kind of like folk songs and stuff better."

"Don't put the boy on the spot," Dr. Knox said. He taught in the math department with Mrs. Hambrick. "Perhaps he just plays the instrument because he likes the way it sounds! Not everything has to do with history, you know."

"Well, we certainly have a great deal of War Between the States history around here," Dr. Seagraves said. She didn't seem mad at Dr. Knox for ribbing her.

"Civil War, if you please," Dr. Knox said, shaking his head. "I've been telling you that all year."

Dr. Seagraves smiled at Dr. Knox and brushed away a strand of black hair that had come loose from her long braid. "If you stay here long enough, Knoxie, you'll get the name straight."

Dr. Knox snorted. "You'd know as much about that as I do. You came here from Missouri!"

"Remember, my family came from North Carolina originally," Dr. Seagraves said, frowning slightly. "They fled after Sherman's raiders destroyed their home."

My eyes widened. I wondered if Dr. Seagraves had family here waiting for her all that time, cousins or great-great-great-great-nieces and -nephews or something. It was over a hundred years since the Civil War—how long did you have to wait for people to come back?

"She's been trying to sort out the family genealogy," Mrs. Hambrick explained.

Dr. Seagraves pushed her plate away. "I got a chance to come here as a visiting professor, but my year's almost up and

I haven't found anything. My mother's grandmother was just a young girl when she left North Carolina after the War. She married a man named Andrew Harkens, but I couldn't find any record of him. Then she died in her twenties after having a baby girl. She could never bring herself to talk about her old home or the rest of her family, and we're not even sure of her maiden name."

Mrs. Hambrick nodded. "So many Southern names were lost after the War. Family lines continued, but it was the women who went on. And it's so hard to trace your ancestors through the female side of the family!"

Dr. Seagraves sighed. "It was foolish to come here expecting to discover hidden family secrets."

I thought about tracing my own family, as a student waiter took away our lunch plates and brought us dessert. I knew Dad's parents had died—I'd seen pictures of them in an old album and pictures of Uncle Greg when he was a kid. There were even old, faded photos of my great-grandparents as kids, looking serious in strange grown-up-style clothes. But I didn't know anything about my mother's family. She had told me everything about families who'd lived thousands of years ago, but nothing about her own. I didn't even know where they lived.

"Dr. Seagraves," I asked hesitantly, "where did you look to learn about your folks?"

Dad glanced at me, surprised, but Mrs. Hambrick smiled, like we were one big happy family already.

"I checked county records," Dr. Seagraves told me, spooning up some purplish sherbet. "But a lot of them were destroyed during the Reconstruction. The ones left in the archives didn't tell me anything. I've also been checking with genealogical societies and the Daughters of the Confederacy, of course."

Dr. Knox looked up from his cheesecake. "I still find it hard to believe that people feel proud of ancestors who fought for the Confederacy. Fighting for the Union, sure—they fought to unite the country and to abolish slavery! It was a noble cause."

Dr. Seagraves shook her head decisively. "Some Northerners certainly wanted to abolish slavery and believed in uniting the country, but the government used the idea to inspire popular support for their political and economic aims."

"Well, defeating the South certainly freed the slaves and reunited the Union," Dr. Knox pointed out.

Dr. Seagraves put her spoon down, spilling a puddle of sherbet onto her plate. "Yes, but it also brought new suffering not just for the soldiers who died on both sides, but for the families that were broken apart and lost track of one another."

"Perhaps something will turn up about your ancestors before the semester ends," Mrs. Hambrick said softly.

Dr. Seagraves smiled. "Well, I appreciate the thought, Paige, but I'm afraid I'll have to go home to St. Louis this summer not knowing. I suppose it sounds silly, but knowing who your family was tells you something about who you are. I wanted to learn that."

I wanted to learn it, too. I pushed away my plate of half-eaten pie. The crust was too sweet, and the syrup stuck in my throat.

Outside, after lunch, the professors spoke together in the quad. I liked the trim hedges and the bright flowers lining the walkways up to the speckled stone buildings.

Dad pulled me aside, down a little walkway and out of ear-shot of the others. "Thanks, Defender of the Galaxy," he said, winking at me. "I appreciate your being so polite to Dr. Seagraves. I owe you one."

I couldn't help smiling at the old nickname, even if it was kind of dumb. Then I thought, If he owes me one, why not collect? "Okay, then tell me about Mom's family. Dr. Seagraves said it's important to know the family you came from. I know about you and your side of the family, but what about Mom?"

He frowned and glanced over his shoulder, but Mrs. Hambrick was still talking with the professors. "This isn't the time or place for this conversation."

"When, then? Why won't you ever talk about her?" I knew I sounded whiny, but I'd tried to have this conversation with him too many times to give up now. He always had some excuse not to tell me any more about Mom than I knew for myself.

Dad shut his eyes. Finally he said, "You want to know about your mother's family?" He kept his voice down, but his round face flushed. "Well, I can't help you. She never gave me a straight answer about where she came from."

"Please, Dad—there aren't any wedding pictures anywhere, or pictures of her parents—I've got to have grandparents somewhere, don't I? Why didn't I ever meet them?"

Dad took a deep breath. "We eloped and got married by a justice of the peace. No fancy wedding, no pictures. She said she didn't want any—she wanted to live the moment, not pose for it with photos. She told me her parents were dead— she didn't have anyone to come to a wedding. I was so carried away that I just believed her." He looked up, and his grey eyes shone with tears. "I don't even know if she was telling the truth, okay? She said her maiden name was Thomson, but she never showed me a picture of her parents or told me where she'd grown up. I wish things were different—believe me, I do—but I don't think she wanted us to be able to find any answers."

I jammed my fists down into my jeans pockets as far as they would go and stared at the pebbly paving on the walkway. Even under the hot sun I felt cold inside. Why hadn't Mom told Dad about her family? I couldn't understand, and it scared me.

"Bill?" Mrs. Hambrick said. "Alexander? Are you two all right?"

Her friends had gone, and she stood there looking concerned. I wanted to tell her, No, I'm not okay, and my dad's not okay, and it's all your fault! But I couldn't say anything.

25

"We were just talking about going to the battlefield tomorrow," Dad told her, blinking hard before he turned away from me.

I could have said I wouldn't go. I could have told Mrs. Hambrick I couldn't care less about her stupid Civil War, or War Between the States, or whatever they wanted to call it. But I remembered the ghosts last night, with their wide-brimmed hats and their rifles glinting in the moonlight. Maybe they were soldiers from the War.

"It's almost the anniversary of the end of the siege of Petersburg," Mrs. Hambrick said, her face relaxing a little. "They have reenactors do living history demonstrations at the battlefield—I'm sure you'll like it, Alexander."

I could feel Dad's eyes on me, willing me to be polite. I just followed Dad and Mrs. Hambrick down the wide wooden steps to the parking lot below as she talked. I wasn't interested in living history shows. I was interested in the ghosts.

Before Mom left, I'd never said anything to Dad about the Indian ghosts I saw. But the first summer after she left, I'd felt the cold and smelled the tang of oranges again. When I found myself shivering in the July heat, I knew I was looking into another window through time.

I saw the grassy Indiana field grow wet in the afternoon sun, until it turned into a swamp, with clear water in the middle and muddy places near the banks. Men led horses across it, men in rusty armor with puffy sleeves, wearing curved helmets on their heads. Some men inched across

26

rickety wooden bridges, swaying above the deepest parts of the water. At the far bank, men tugged at the horses, knee-deep in sticky mud. I was so excited, I ran and told Dad, and he smiled at me, the bluish light from his computer monitor turning his face pale.

"I can almost see the soldiers the way you describe them," he said. "De Soto's men, right? Where did you hear about them?"

"I didn't hear about them," I tried to tell him. "They're there—you can see them if you don't mind the cold. It's like looking through a window. Mom said I could see ghosts!"

His face closed up then, crumpling like a spelling test littered with mistakes. "Was that a game you two played?" His voice sounded rusty. Then he swallowed and said, "It sounds like fun."

"It's not a game—I saw them!"

"Okay, Defender of the Galaxy," he said dully. "I'm sure you did." But as he turned back to his computer, I knew he didn't believe me. When I ran outside again, the soldiers were gone and the swamp had turned back into a dry grassy plain. I felt so sad at losing them I couldn't stop the tears from leaking down my cheeks.

I asked the school librarian, and she said De Soto had crossed the swamp in Busseron Creek Valley and camped at Merom on his way to Terre Haute. He was looking for a road to the South Sea so they could get to China. But I didn't know why I'd seen them, or the Indians before them. I hadn't found any more windows through time since then—until last night.

I thought about going to the battlefield tomorrow. If that was where the soldiers were headed, maybe that's why I'd had to make this trip to North Carolina—not because Dad liked Mrs. Hambrick, but so I could find out about the ghosts.

Chapter Three

THE SIEGE OF PETERSBURG

"Where were you?" demanded Carleton as I opened the front door on Saturday morning.

I could see Mrs. Hambrick frowning over his shoulder and Nicole smirking. Dad didn't say anything.

"I was out running," I told them, as if they couldn't tell from my sweaty clothes. "I run every morning. Dad knows. Usually he runs with me."

"I thought I told you we were planning on an early start today," Dad said.

"Well, everybody was still snoring when I went out, so I didn't figure you were starting *that* early."

"Just get cleaned up," Dad told me.

I went into the bathroom and took my time doing my cooldowns before getting into the shower. Then I pulled on jeans and a T-shirt, with the blue-and-grey plaid shirt hanging open this time, tied the lariat around my wrist, and headed down to the kitchen to see what was for breakfast.

"Hurry up, Alexander!" Dad called impatiently from the driveway. "Paige said to grab something to eat and just bring it with you."

I glanced out the window. He and Mrs. Hambrick were studying a map, and her kids were already sitting in a beat-up old van that looked as dingy as the house itself. I grabbed a few slices of bread, slathered on some peanut butter and marmalade, and headed outside.

Nicole was sprawled out, taking the whole rear seat of the van. Carleton was bouncing up and down in the seat in front of her, and the grown-ups obviously had dibs on the front seat.

"Move over," I told Nicole.

She shook her head.

"I get sick unless I sit in the backseat," I told her. "I tend to throw up. Not that anything could hurt this wreck, but it kind of stinks, you know?"

Nicole studied me. "That's bull. Sitting in the backseat makes people sick."

I shook my head. "Other people, maybe. Not me." I shrugged. "Well, it's not your problem. Yet." I started to climb in next to Carleton.

"Eeuuwwhh! I don't want you barfing on me!" he cried. "Sit in the back."

I turned to Nicole, and she reluctantly made a little room on the seat.

"Excuse me," I said, climbing over her. "I need to sit by the window. That way I can open it if I start feeling—you know, queasy." A blob of marmalade slid out of one of the sandwiches and missed her knee by less than an inch.

"Gross!" She slid past me and moved up next to Carleton.

Dad climbed in the front passenger seat. "You guys okay back there?"

I held my breath. Nicole tightened her seat belt but didn't say anything. After a quick glance at her, Carleton said, "Yeah, we're okay."

I'd counted on Nicole not wanting to talk to Dad any more than she absolutely had to. If she'd said anything, I'd have been stuck in the smaller front seat in a heartbeat. Dad knows I never get carsick, no matter what I've been eating.

I settled back to enjoy the ride.

"I'm really looking forward to seeing the battlefield," Mrs. Hambrick said, after we'd been on I-85 heading north for a while. "I can't believe we live this close to Petersburg and we've never driven up to see it."

"That's because no one was interested, Mother," Nicole said in a bored voice.

"I imagine you'll be more interested when you get there," Mrs. Hambrick told her. "The city of Petersburg was besieged by Union troops for nine whole months! Both sides actually dug trenches in the earth and then built up earthworks, with sharpened sticks pointing out toward the other line in order to stop a charge. Soldiers could stand in the trenches and shoot over the tops of barricades made of dirt."

"Cool," Carleton said. "Can I build a trench in the backyard?"

"We don't need a trench," his mother told him. "We don't have any soldiers besieging us."

"Why were the soldiers in Petersburg?" asked Carleton.

"Who cares?" muttered Nicole.

"Come on," Dad said. "This is interesting."

"Yeah," said Carleton, elbowing his sister.

Nicole shrugged. "We never went to any battlefields, because Dad thought they were boring."

No one said anything for a minute. I actually felt sorry for Nicole—maybe she missed her dad the way I missed Mom. Of course, it wasn't the same thing. He couldn't ever come back.

Mrs. Hambrick said, "Well, there were plenty of things your father liked that you thought were boring. Remember the time he took you to see an opera and you fell asleep?" She looked into her rearview mirror. The way it was angled, I think she could see Nicole.

Nicole kind of shrugged.

"Your father didn't mind it when you liked different things than he did," her mother said softly.

Nicole just stared out the window.

Yeah, stick to your guns, I thought. You don't have to believe her.

"So why were the soldiers in Petersburg?" Carleton asked again.

Mrs. Hambrick was quiet for a minute, still looking at Nicole in the mirror. Then she said, "Petersburg protected the railroad line that went straight up to Richmond, the capital of the Confederacy." Now she sounded more like she was a teacher talking to a class. "In the end, the war came down to a question of whether or not General Lee, the Southern commander, could keep General Grant and the Northern Army out of Petersburg and away from the railroad."

"Why didn't that general just go around Petersburg and take another road?" Carleton asked.

"There wasn't another road, you moron," Nicole said. "They couldn't just jump in a car like this, you know."

"Actually, there were other ways to get to Richmond," Mrs. Hambrick began.

"See? I told you!" Carleton crowed.

"But Grant had tried every way, and Lee's Army always blocked him. So Grant decided to dig his own earthworks at Petersburg and wait out the Confederate Army. He could get food and supplies for the Union Army, but Lee's men only had what food and medicines and supplies they carried with them, or could get in the city itself. Everyone—even old men and young boys—fought in the siege, trying to protect the city, but there were just too many Union soldiers. General Grant captured Petersburg."

She sounded sad, as if it hadn't happened so long ago, and I thought about those tired-looking ghosts. Were they really struggling to get to Petersburg? It was too late for them to change what had happened at the siege. Did ghosts keep doing the same thing even though they knew it wasn't going to change anything, just because they'd done it in real life? Why be a ghost and show yourself to people unless something could be changed?

At the battlefield, I let Nicole and Carleton climb out before jumping down myself. I rubbed my stomach and tried to look sick, but Nicole just rolled her eyes and started off for the building.

"Where's the trenches and the earth-i-cades?" asked Carleton. "No, that's not it—the earth—what were they?"

"Earthworks, cretin," Nicole told him. "Or barricades. Take your pick—but not both at once."

I tried not to grin, but Carleton was kind of cute. He looked at me, and I winked. He laughed and ran over to his mother.

"First we get the map for the driving tour," she said, leading the way to a long, low building off to one side of the parking lot. "That's where you'll see the trenches and the earthworks."

I rolled up the flannel sleeves of my shirt, since it had warmed up, and followed my dad. He glanced over his shoulder and smiled at me, but I just looked intently at the sleeve I was working on. I didn't want him to think I was having a good time.

Inside I saw a gift shop that looked like a library at first, it had so many books. I passed those by while Mrs. Hambrick got some maps. I went up a ramp to a round building with real uniforms and rifled muskets, and displays showing ramrods and paper cartridges with powder and minié balls—that's what they shot then, instead of bullets. I saw some weapons that looked like stubby metal tubes on a flat base. The sign said they were called Coehorn mortars, and they worked kind of like little cannon.

I looked at a drawing of a line of earthworks with deep zigzagging trenches. Soldiers on the enemy line would be firing Coehorn mortars back into your trenches. What would it be like to stand behind those earthworks while someone was shooting hollow iron balls filled with gunpowder at you from a mortar? I shivered, thinking of those soldiers who had held Petersburg for nine months.

"Hey—no you don't!" Dad said.

I looked over one shoulder and saw an opening in the floor that showed a fake trench leading to sort of a burrow dug out of the earth with a hard plank roof—the sign said it was a bomb proof, where soldiers could rest when they were off duty. That little wooden roof was supposed to keep them safe from the shelling. Carleton was halfway under the display railing before Dad grabbed him.

"But I want to see the trench!" Carleton complained.

"Sure you do, pal—but not here, okay?" Dad told him.

I turned away, sorry I'd winked, and headed into a room in the center of the round building. It turned out to be an auditorium, and I saw a model of the town of Petersburg and the countryside. We were just in time to catch the next show—a taped talk with lights flashing on the model showing the armies and the way the battle shifted. The prerecorded lecture explained that things got steadily worse for the Confederate Army in 1865, until General Gordon proposed a desperate plan to break the siege. His soldiers would cut a path in the night to the Union earthworks at a place called Fort Stedman. At dawn they would launch a surprise attack. And it worked! But Gordon's troops couldn't hold Fort Stedman. He managed to get some of his men back to safety only because a unit of North Carolina soldiers covered the retreat.

I felt my chest tighten as the lights showed the Southern line being pushed back, as Lee pulled his army out and let Petersburg fall, as Grant pursued him. Then Lee surrendered, and I finally released the breath I'd been holding as the lights went out.

Chapter Four

STEADFAST TO THE LAST

"Wow," Carleton said softly, actually subdued for once. I guess he'd figured out that those trenches and bomb proofs weren't just for fun.

"So—where do we go from here?" Nicole asked, getting up and turning her back on the model.

"Can we see Fort Stedman?" I heard myself asking. Why couldn't I keep my mouth shut? I really hadn't wanted to show any interest in any part of the battlefield. But something about that story got to me. Those guys made a last-ditch effort—and they failed. And so many of them died.

"It's on the driving tour," Mrs. Hambrick said.

Outside, a National Parks guard gave us a list of the living history demonstrations.

"Can we see a real cannon shoot?" Carleton asked, wide-eyed. "And climb into a real trench?"

The guard just smiled as my dad kept a firm grip on Carleton's hand.

We climbed back into the van, and I claimed the backseat with no trouble. But I didn't feel any sense of victory. I just sat there, staring outside and thinking of those guys struggling to cover the retreat from Fort Stedman. Old men and boys, Mrs. Hambrick had said. Why would a kid do that? What was he trying to hold on to that he'd stand there holding Fort Stedman to the last? It scared me just thinking about it.

The driving trail wound through different places on the battlefield. The ground on either side of the road was thick with dead leaves and old, dried grass, and you could see the strange way the surface rose and dipped.

"I don't see any trenches," Carleton complained.

"Look closer," my dad told him. "Can you see those waves in the ground? It looks like rolling land, but it's really man-made. There are your trenches."

"Now I see," Carleton said, staring at them.

I could see what Dad was talking about, too. But Nature had softened the curves. It was difficult to imagine how those trenches would have carved up the land into opposing lines of earthworks that the soldiers had depended on to save their lives during the War. I almost expected to see the ghosts from last night standing in the trenches, but there was no one.

Then the driving tour wound past a curve in the road, and I saw what those earthworks were all about. This stop on the tour was a maze of reconstructed zigzagging trenches that showed the front line's firing steps inside the earthworks and the sharpened stakes pointing toward the enemy line. I saw signs saying Keep Off Earthworks on the trenches, and the parking lot was jammed. One of the living history demonstrations was going on in front of some log buildings and a canvas tent. But it looked like marching and drilling—no cannon for Carleton.

"Let's try the next one," Dad suggested.

So we drove on through the shadows of pin oaks and live oaks. All around I could see grass and ferns growing over the remains of the original entrenchments. The trees that grew back then would have been cut down to make planks for bomb proofs, and the branches used for those sharpened stakes, or to build fires to keep soldiers warm. I shuddered at the thought of all those living trees destroyed so that people could fight.

Then the road suddenly opened up and there was a huge parking lot. I could see a cannon and a crew of reenactors in blue uniforms off to the right, with horses harnessed to a two-wheeled wagon. People crowded around them, but there were still places in the parking lot, so Mrs. Hambrick pulled in. A paved path curved away west toward the trees, to the left of the uniformed soldiers with their cannon.

As soon as his mom turned off the engine, Carleton was out of the van, shouting, "It really *is* a cannon!" Nicole climbed out and looked around like she was trying to make a statement in boredom. But I saw her glancing from the cannon to the curving path, and I remembered her hurry to get out of the auditorium. I thought she was more shaken by the story of the siege of Petersburg than she wanted to admit.

"They're still setting up," I told Dad, who was already starting off after Carleton. "I'm going to explore—I'll be back before anything happens."

He glanced up at me, but I started off, sure he wouldn't come with me. He was too busy keeping an eye on Mrs. Hambrick's son to worry about his own. I was afraid Nicole would follow, but no shoes hit the pavement except mine.

Behind me, I heard the excited buzz of voices and the creak of leather and metal as the horses shifted in their harnesses. But the grassy plain was quiet in the spring morning. March 25—the same day that Gordon's men had charged Fort Stedman. I felt a shiver of anticipation go through me, and then I broke free of the plain and turned off into a small shaded area surrounded by a rail fence. There were signs on the other side of the rails saying Keep Off Earthworks, and I thought how disappointed Carleton would be when he saw that the same signs were everywhere.

I was a little disappointed myself. I'd been hoping to see the ghosts once I got away from everyone, but there was nothing here at all, except a lone artillery piece and a sign saying this was Colquitt's Salient, the farthest forward part of the Con-federate line. This was the place where Gordon's men were when he thought they could break through the Union line.

I turned and sighted along the artillery piece to the crowd of people gathered at the cannon. Dad and the Hambricks must be among them. I could just make out the rise in the land to the right, where the low mound of Fort Stedman sat. It wasn't such a long walk—but in the night, creeping forward, trying not to tip off the Union troops while you were cutting away the stakes in front of their earthworks, it must have seemed farther away than the moon.

I started back, following the line of the Confederate advance. Artillery pieces sat in front of the fort, pointing straight at me. The path dipped a little, then came up on a rise.

I heard the reenactors shouting orders over by the cannon, and I heard someone squeal in excitement—Carleton? But I kept on going, into the fort. I expected to see sharply dug zigzagging trenches, but the ground sank gently away from the marked pathways, then rose to the outer earthworks, with a fuzz of spring grass softening the curves. I glanced over my shoulder, but the outer earthworks blocked the cannon demonstration.

I turned to look at the sunken ground. Would there have been firing steps down there, where a soldier could stand and shoot at the attackers? Or was that depression a bomb proof? Perhaps planking had covered the soldiers who huddled there when they had a chance to rest. Or could an artillery piece have sat there, braced against the dirt as it shot over the earthworks at the Confederate lines?

I took a step forward. I heard a shout behind me and thought for a panicky moment that a Parks guard must have caught me climbing around where I wasn't allowed, but no one was there. The voice had come from one of the soldiers at the living history demonstration.

"Gunner! Load cannister!"

I turned back to the sunken ground of Fort Stedman. What had it felt like to be down there with the mortar shells bursting around you?

"Infantry at three hundred yards!"

I took another step forward, past the Keep Off Earthworks sign.

"Hold your ears now!"

I took another step, and the rubber sole of my running shoe slipped on the grass. I felt myself sliding into the sunken hole, which was much deeper than I had expected.

"Fire!"

I heard a terrible explosion, and suddenly I smelled bitter orange and felt mud and icy water sloshing over my feet as I flailed for balance at the bottom of the hole.

"Again!" The voice sounded louder and hoarse from shouting.

The sunny day had gone overcast and cold, and I wasn't alone anymore. Then a terrific explosion went off just in front of me, and I saw a cannon rolling backward toward me. I fell away from it, jamming both hands over my ears.

"Here, you! Get down!" Unexpectedly cold hands shoved me into a depression in the dirt, partially covered by rough wooden planks.

I could make out a steady drumming sound, and over it I heard popping noises, almost like kernels of popcorn in a microwave, but much louder and lower pitched.

"Good shot, Chamblee!" a man's voice called out.

I heard chuffing sounds right over my head. Then I heard more of those strange popping noises in front of me, deep and whooshing, while the beating kept up a steady rhythm. I looked up through the haze of smoke, shivering and terrified. To my left, I saw a boy standing with a drum that dangled from his hip almost all the way down to his ankle. The kid was younger than me but older than Carleton, and he didn't look as if he was having any fun playing in the earthworks. His face was streaked with dirt and looked dead serious. He kept hammering his drumsticks on the drumhead in an unending rolling sound as if his life depended on it.

In front of me, standing inside the earthworks that should have looked out on the parking lot, I could see a group of dirty men in worn brown or grey coats standing with muskets. One man rammed a long rod down the barrel of his musket, while another held his own higher, fiddling with something on the side of the gun, near the trigger. I couldn't see anything like a parking lot beyond the men, just a muddy space stretching away into smoky haze.

A younger soldier already had his long musket up to his shoulder, and I jumped as the popping whoosh went off when he fired. Another chuffing sound like a steam engine rushed past my head, and I turned and saw a man fall. I realized that the noise was the sound of a minié ball shot into the fort! I crouched lower, hugging the ground in desperation, but I could still see the soldiers. Could I be shot by a ghost minié ball? There was no window protecting me from the past anymore—I was part of that time, and I wished I'd never stepped into the earthworks.

The boy continued to beat his drum in that steady roll as the soldiers in front of him kept shooting. The young soldier reached down into a leather pouch, pulled out a paper cartridge, then tore it open with his teeth. He poured the powder down the muzzle, then pushed in the minié ball and used his ramrod to shove it down the barrel. He rested the ramrod against something shiny stuck in the ground, then he pulled back the hammer and jammed a little copper-colored metal cap in place and fired again.

"They're falling back!" a voice shouted.

"Cease fire! Cease fire on the line!" the first man's hoarse voice rang out. Then, much louder in the sudden stillness, he called, "Boy!"

I jerked my head around, thinking for a panicky moment that he was shouting at me. I saw a man in a uniform with a high collar, with mud-splattered gold braid on his shoulders—probably an officer. But he wasn't calling me. The drummer boy ran forward, the large drum banging awk-wardly against his hip.

"A Company, B Company, C Company, fall back!" the officer yelled. "Back to the salient! Carry what wounded you can."

I saw grubby-looking men in threadbare grey uniforms climbing over the earthworks behind me. Some of them didn't even have on real uniforms—they were just wearing shirts and ragged brownish-colored jackets. The earth walls were much higher than I expected, towering above me, with sodden sand-bags piled on top. In front of me, the shooters I'd seen reloaded their muskets and waited, except for the younger one, who jumped down. I saw him bend over a body on the ground, then fumble for a leather box around the man's waist and pull out a fistful of paper cartridges. He shoved them into his own box. Then he took out a handful of something smaller—those copper-colored caps I'd seen him use—and stuck them into a different pouch on his belt. He moved to another fallen man and reached into his cartridge box.

The drummer boy snapped to attention in front of the officer with the gold braid.

"Drummer boy, fall back with A, B, and C Companies of the 49th," the officer told him. "Find General Gordon and tell him that D, E, and I Companies will hold them one more time, then fall back. He must fire the Coehorn mortars just east of this fort to cover our retreat. Do you understand, boy? Repeat the order!"

"But, sir," the boy stammered. "Who will beat the long roll? I'm the last drummer boy left."

The officer's face softened. "That's all right, son. The men know what to do. And it is critical the message be carried faithfully. Now repeat the order."

"Yes, sir," the boy said, twisting the drumsticks. "A, B, and C Companies of the 49th falling back. D, E, and I Companies will hold the Yanks one more time, then fall back. Fire the Coehorn mortars at—at—"

"Just east of Stedman," the man repeated.

"Yes, sir," the boy said quickly. "Fire the Coehorn mortars just east of Stedman to cover the retreat!"

The officer nodded. "Go now."

The boy saluted, hauled himself up over the earthworks, and raced across the ragged remains of a cornfield to carry the message.

Through a shooting gap, I saw the retreating men stumbling across the cornfield I'd crossed just a few moments ago in my own time, when it was a grassy plain. The soldiers pulled the wounded along through the broken stalks of corn toward safety, sometimes staggering and using their muskets to keep on their feet. Every few seconds I could hear those popping sounds, softer in the distance. I pushed myself under the planks as far as I could go, terrified—freezing—helpless, and wanting to cry.

"Go on." A cold boot prodded me impatiently, and I could feel the chill cut through my shirt as if someone had dropped an ice cube down my back. "Get on back to the salient before they come again."

I looked up into a dirt-streaked face barely older than my own. Old men and young boys, Mrs. Hambrick had said. This was one of the boys—the one who had been checking the bodies. Apparently my jeans and the plaid shirt blended in well enough with the variety of uniforms that he just thought I was another soldier.

I shook my head at him. I don't belong here, I wanted to tell him, but I couldn't find my voice.

The boy's eyes widened—they were the black wells I had seen in the mist the first night at the Hambricks'. "You're—not one of us," he said.

For a moment I thought the boy was going to swing his long musket around and point it at me. Then he reached out a grimy hand. "You're an out-of-timer! But you're in my time now, and you see me—thank God! I've been praying for someone all these years. You must help me!"

"Chamblee," the officer said, moving closer to where I was hiding, and the boy whirled around, blocking me from sight. "Out of ammunition?"

"Yes, sir," the boy said, standing stiffly. "Replenishing it for their next assault, sir, but there's not much left."

The officer nodded. "You shoot faster and straighter than any other soldier, Chamblee." His voice sounded tired. "I wish I had a thousand men like you and an ammunition wagon. Then we'd push those Yankees back—and keep them back."

"We'll hold them, sir!" the boy said.

The officer smiled at him a little sadly. He must realize what was going to happen, I thought. That's why he sent some of his men back. He knew they would lose Fort Stedman. And what would happen to me when the fort was retaken?

"Yes, we'll hold them one more time, Private Chamblee," he said.

A voice called, "I see them forming up, sir! They're about four hundred yards out!"

The officer glanced to the east of Fort Stedman. "Back to your position now, Private," he said, and his voice had turned decisive.

"Chamblee! Come on, lad!" I looked up at the firing steps inside the earthworks and saw an older man beckoning.

The boy glanced down at me as he started toward the earthworks. "Don't forget," he said in a low voice. "Help me!"

Then he grabbed the older man's hand and pulled himself up with the others.

"Steady now!" the officer called. "Set your sights at three hundred yards!"

The Union troops were attacking. What did the boy mean, to help him?

"Front rank!" the officer cried. "Fire!"

I heard the popping sounds ripple across the line—louder this time.

"Second rank! Fire!"

I also heard that chuffing sound again, rushing over my head.

"Fire at will!" the officer shouted. Then I heard something like the thumping sound your knuckles make when you rap on a watermelon. When I looked back at him, the officer had fallen and the dirt around him was turning a muddy red color.

The popping got louder, so many shots blurring together that they blended into a deafening sound like the roar of the surf. I saw the older soldier fall. The boy glanced down at him for a second, his face stricken, as he reloaded. Then he stepped sideways, standing over the fallen man, swung his musket to his shoulder, and fired again. He pulled out a new cartridge and was biting into the paper even before the smoke at the muzzle cleared.

The surf roared ceaselessly around me. The boy rested his ramrod against the metal object in the dirt so he could load faster. He fired and loaded and fired again, his body moving in a steady rhythm. The men around him fired and fumbled for reloads, and finally the surf sound sputtered out into separate pops as men ran out of ammunition, or turned and ran back toward the salient, or died.

The boy kept firing until his hand reached for a cartridge and came away empty. He froze for a second, then looked down at the man beneath him as if to say good-bye. He reached for his ramrod and shoved it into place under the barrel of his musket, then grabbed the metal object from the dirt. Now I could see it was a long bayonet with a deadly three-sided blade. The boy twisted it onto the muzzle just as a wave of blue uniforms swept over the eastern wall of Fort Stedman. He charged toward the officer leading the attack, a high, shrill yell of defiance coming from him. The officer stumbled back, pointing. Five or six of the men in blue threw their muskets up to their shoulders and shot the young soldier.

The explosion deafened me.

Then I heard the soft patter of distant clapping.

I sat up. There was no mud, and the jagged trenches were only soft grassy depressions in the sunny battlefield park. I felt tears burn my eyes, the relief was so strong, and then the sense of loss hit me. Unsteadily, I got to my feet. I could hear footsteps, and I scrambled out of the sunken ground I'd slid into and back onto the path before the guards and the tourists who had been watching the living history demonstration got close enough to see me.

Why had that boy asked for my help?

Somehow I'd shattered the window through time and fallen into the past, and it was worse than anything I had ever imagined.

Chapter Five

PRIVATE RICHESON FRANCIS CHAMBLEE

"You missed it all!" Carleton shouted, running into the fort. "There was this big cannon—POW! And then they did it again—POW! And the blue soldiers charged out like they were chasing the grey soldiers all the way home!"

"What's with you?" Nicole asked. "You look like you've seen a ghost."

I jerked a little, and she smirked.

"Or maybe that delicate stomach of yours is getting ready to throw up your breakfast. Good—do it out here instead of in the van."

I turned away. I did feel kind of clammy and sick, and I didn't know how to hide it. I thought I'd wanted to see ghosts again, but that was before I'd had minié balls whizzing over my head and cannon going off by my ear.

"Are you okay, Alexander?" Mrs. Hambrick asked.

"What's wrong?" Dad asked, hurrying over.

I shook my head. I sure couldn't tell him I'd seen more ghosts. "Nothing—I'm just a little hot after hiking over to Colquitt's Salient, that's all. I'm going to sit in the van, in the shade, okay?"

Mrs. Hambrick gave me the keys, and I walked back to the parking lot. I unlocked the van and climbed into the middle seat, leaving the door open so some air could get in. It was cool in spite of the heat outside. In fact, it was chilly. After sitting in the sun in the parking lot, the van was strangely cold.

I turned around, feeling my throat tighten. The boy stared back at me from the rear seat, his black eyes huge in his thin, pale face. He was lean and hard—I hadn't realized how thin he was during the fighting in Fort Stedman, maybe because all the soldiers looked nearly starved. He floated a little way above the seat, as if he were sitting on a cushion of air, half propped against the roll of blankets strapped to his back. A small canvas knapsack lay beside him, the strap dangling from his shoulder. He held a tall musket, the sunlight running down the steel of that long, three-sided bayonet fastened onto the side of it. The blade came to a sharp point.

"Hello, out-of-timer," the boy said softly, and his voice sounded tired.

I opened my mouth to say something, but nothing came out. I mean—here it was, a real ghost! I should have been thrilled he was actually talking to me. I should be pounding him with questions. But I stared at that musket with its bayonet and remembered the sound of the bullets, and I couldn't say a word. He was just too real. Seeing the Indians and De Soto's men had been exciting—because they hadn't seen me. But this ghost was here with me! What if the Union soldiers followed him through the window?

"No," I finally managed to say. Staying on the outside—watching an echo of something play itself out after it was all over and done with—that was one thing. But being right in the middle of it, getting shot at—it wasn't *my* war! "Go away," I whispered unsteadily.

He shook his head slowly. "My name's Chamblee," he said in a low drawl. "Richeson Francis Chamblee, Private Chamblee, in D Company of the 49th, pleased to make your acquaintance. I have been waiting a long time for an out-of-timer to see me. Now, what's your name, friend?"

"I'm not your friend!" I practically shouted. "I'm not seeing this."

"But you *are* seeing me, Red," he told me, his eyes going up to my hair and his mouth curving into a faint smile. "That's how I know you were sent to help me. And I truly need your help."

I slid off the seat and out of the van.

"I wasn't 'sent' to help anybody," I muttered. "I've got my own problems."

A cool shadow fell across the corner of the parking lot where I was standing.

"Then perhaps we can help each other." Private Chamblee stood beside me, floating an inch or so above the pavement, one hand gripping his musket.

"No!" I shook my head and jammed my shaking fists into my pockets. "I can't help you. I'm sorry! Just go back to Fort Stedman!"

"But that's not where I belong, Red," he said, his voice harder. "I never belonged up here in Virginia! I belong at Two Stirrups. That's why I need your help."

What kind of a crazy name was Two Stirrups? I didn't want to know. I remembered him lunging at the officer with his bayonet, and my eyes slid away from the sun reflecting off the blade on the musket he still held tightly. "Then—go back to Two Stirrups if that's where you belong!"

"Two Stirrups is gone now," he said. "Burned by the Yanks. I should have been there, not here. I should have stopped Sherman's raiders!"

I saw Carleton running toward us. Dad followed a little way behind with Mrs. Hambrick. "Look—just go away before they get here!" I told him.

The ghost laughed, a dusty laugh that didn't sound as if the boy found anything much funny. "Why?" he drawled. "Those other out-of-timers—they can't see me. No one has, since the War. You're the only one, Red."

I shivered and swallowed hard, almost pleased for an instant, even though I wanted him to leave me alone.

"Are you going to throw up?" Carleton asked, suspicious.

The ghost chuckled.

"No!" I snapped. I was saying "no" to the ghost, too, but he didn't seem to care.

"Good," said Carleton, climbing into the van.

"Okay, we've seen Petersburg," said Nicole. "Can we go now?"

"Is that your sister?" the ghost asked, with a strange emphasis on the word *sister*. "What's her name?" He'd stopped asking for help—now he sounded almost envious.

"No," I muttered.

"Who put you in charge?" Nicole said, glaring at me. The ghost was right—they couldn't see him. But they could sure hear me talking to him!

"Is she promised to you, then?" The ghost sounded respectful—but now I really did want to throw up. Me and Nicole?

I closed my eyes and clamped my mouth shut, refusing to answer anybody.

"Come on, kids," said Mrs. Hambrick, coming up. "Back in the van—let's see the rest of this battlefield! May I have the keys, Alexander?"

"Ah, Alexander," drawled the ghost. "So that's who you are, Red. I'm pleased to know you. And is this lady your mother?"

I'd opened my eyes and held out the keys to Mrs. Hambrick. Now I practically shouted, "No!" The keys fell from my hand.

"What?" She stepped back, surprised.

"I meant—" I shook my head. "I'm sorry I dropped your keys! I didn't mean to do that." I stooped, grabbed the keys, and put them in her hand. "I'm really sorry," I repeated, feeling the flush burning my ears.

I'd meant to keep my mouth shut, but I couldn't let that ghost think Mrs. Hambrick was my mom. I climbed into the rear seat, not meeting Dad's eyes when he settled down in the front of the van and glanced at me. I just wanted to get out of here and leave the ghost behind in Fort Stedman.

"Red—Alexander—you've got to believe me!"

I heard the pleading in his voice, but I stared outside and refused to look at him.

"What is it? Why are you afraid of me?" I tightened my lips, not wanting him to know how scared I was. I could see the reflection of him clutching his musket in the window, and his hollow, grimy face looked confused. He studied his own reflection in the glass for a moment, then his eyes widened. "Is it this?"

He reached for the bayonet, and I felt my stomach lurch. Then he twisted the long triangular blade, pulled it off, and slid it into a scabbard on his belt. "I'm not your enemy, Alexander," he said quietly. "But I do need your help."

He looked less dangerous without the bayonet on his musket, but I still didn't want him there. Ghosts should stay on the other side of the window through time, where they belonged. I thought as hard as I could, *Disappear!*

Mrs. Hambrick started the van and backed it out. In front of me, I saw Nicole curling the ends of her hair around her fingers. "Is it cold in here?" she asked.

Mrs. Hambrick frowned. "It does feel chilly, doesn't it?"

"It's a nice change from the heat at the living history show," Dad said.

That set Carleton off describing every detail of the cannon demonstration and silenced everyone else.

In the back, I shivered and rolled down the sleeves of my flannel shirt, wishing I had my old sweatshirt with me. Come on, I thought, willing Mrs. Hambrick to drive faster and get us out of the Fort Stedman area. I was sure I'd feel warmer once we got farther away.

We drove past more earthworks on the right, and then past the next Union fort. A wooden bridge led across the earthworks to a shadowy clump of pine trees. Artillery pieces pointed back toward Fort Stedman and the Confederate line beyond.

I could still feel the cold. I rubbed my arms through the flannel sleeves and tuned out the conversation as Carleton babbled on about the cannon and rattled off so many questions that nobody could get in a word to answer them. Why could I see ghosts? Any ghosts? Those Indians, or De Soto's men, or these Civil War ghosts? Why me? And why could that boy—Richeson Chamblee, or whatever he called himself—why could he see me?

The road sloped upward, and we drove past a ruined brick chimney on the right. I turned away from it and looked at the trees through the left-hand window. Beside the shadowy image of my own face in the glass, I saw another face. It flickered a little, but I recognized the black hair and those hollow eyes staring at me. And then it hit me. I was still cold because the ghost hadn't stayed behind at Fort Stedman. He was here in the van beside me.

I felt sorry I'd done such a good job of making Nicole and Carleton leave me in the rear seat alone. Right then, I wished I were sitting right up front, as near my dad as I could get.

As if he could read my thoughts, the ghost smiled slowly. He said in his soft drawl, "I'm sticking with you, Alexander, like a burr on a horse, until you help me."

I shook my head, just a little, so no one would notice—none of the live people in the van anyway.

The ghost sighed. "I stood on a siege line outside of Petersburg for nearly four months, Red. I guess I can lay siege to you if I have to."

I closed my eyes as the van jounced over some railroad tracks and headed to the last stop in the driving tour. I refused to look at the determination in the boy's face any longer. The sun was hot as I climbed out of the van and followed the others along a row of monuments and commemorative chunks of rock, but it was all I could do to force myself not to shiver, because the ghost walked beside me, every step of the way.

Chapter Six

HAUNTED

"Are you feeling okay, Alexander?" Dad asked when we got back to the Hambricks' house. "You keep shivering—are you coming down with something?" He looked worried. If I got sick, it would spoil his visit with Mrs. Hambrick.

That almost sounded like a good idea—but if he thought I was sick, he'd call a doctor, and no doctor would be able to diagnose a haunting. I'd be the boy with the mysterious chills, poked and prodded by everyone in the Duke University Medical Center. Bad idea.

"Just a little tired," I told him. "Maybe I ran too far this morning."

"Why don't you turn in early?" Mrs. Hambrick asked.

"Yeah," I said. "Maybe I will."

We'd stopped for fast food on the road, but I'd only picked at my chicken nuggets. It was one thing for ghosts to be a special secret between me and Mom—it was another thing to have a ghost following me around that no one else could see. I'd closed my eyes in the van to avoid seeing his reflection in the window, but I still felt a cold draft on my neck. At least he'd toned it down so the others didn't seem to notice the chill as much.

I wondered if I'd still feel cold upstairs. I could get into bed, though, and maybe he wouldn't bother me while I slept.

He climbed the stairs right behind me, trailing his musket, which made a ghostly thunk as if it bumped each step on the way up, even though it floated above them. "You've got a fine home, Alexander. Overgrown garden, though—why don't you and your family tend it better?"

I went into Carleton's room and closed the door behind me. "It's not my house, and they're not my family," I said, even though I didn't want to talk to him.

"Who are they, then?" he asked, standing at the foot of my bed. "Where do you live? You're not at all like the other out-of-timers—your traveling here cannot have been by accident."

I tried to concentrate on fumbling through my duffel bag for my sweatshirt, but I couldn't help wondering. "What do you mean—out-of-timers?"

"I'm set in my time in Fort Stedman," he explained. "Other people come and go, from different times: out-of-timers. They see the fort, and they sometimes even pause as if they sense the battle, but they are not part of my time. You're an out-of-timer, but you were able to witness the battle. You're not like the others."

I shivered as the terror of the battle flashed across my mind. I quickly pulled the sweatshirt on and tucked my hands inside its baggy sleeves.

The ghost looked at the rainbow-striped logo on the front of the shirt and laughed a little uneasily. "That's a funny-colored apple," he said.

How could you explain an Apple computer to a ghost from 1865? I didn't bother trying. I just kicked off my running shoes and climbed into bed. I didn't think he'd hurt me, and I had to do something to get warm. Besides, sleeping would be a good way to get away from him.

In a sudden gust of icy air, the dinosaur wind chime loudly clattered against the glass windowpane. "What are these creatures?" the ghost asked. "Dragons?"

"Dinosaurs," I muttered sleepily, "and computers. You're the out-of-timer, Richeson."

I slipped my hands out of the sweatshirt sleeves long enough to pull the dinosaur quilt up as high as I could, then stuck my head under the pillow, hoping to muffle his response. If he made one, I didn't hear it.

Huddling under the covers, I drew my knees up to my chest, trying to hang on to every degree of heat I could. My head ached from the bitter orange tang nobody else could smell, and my eyes felt dry and gritty. I twisted in Carleton's extra bed, tugging the dinosaur quilt closer around me, but I couldn't seem to get warm.

I stand in bone-chilling water and my running shoes are no protection at all. I wish I had my snow boots. First it snows, then it sleets, and then it rains. I play cribbage on a handmade board under a plank roof while the sleet hammers on the boards above my head—which feels weird, because I've never played cribbage in my life. It's one of those games you hear about that only old people play. But now I know all the moves.

I shuffle a deck of playing cards, the stiffness all worn out of them and the faces softened and rubbed to the point where I can hardly see the difference between diamonds and hearts in the smoky oil light. I listen to distant voices—not ghosts—real voices, reading poetry and novels of gallant soldiers and ladyloves left at home. And always in the background, I hear the roar of cannon and smell the smoke.

Sometimes I stand ankle-deep in icy water, hoisting a heavy shovel full of frozen dirt. Sometimes I march, my numbed feet stamping the ground in time with the other soldiers. In between moments of snowy camaraderie with the others, I see glimpses of a farmhouse with a neat front lawn and beds of bright flowers circling the wide veranda of the freshly painted house—white walls, with a dark green door and matching green shutters at the windows. I hear laughter—a girl's laughter. And I hear a father's voice—stern, but laughing, too. I don't hear a mother's voice, though. I feel something damp on my cheek and wonder if I'm crying because my mother's gone, even in my dreams.

"Why did you sleep with your clothes on?"

I blinked at the daylight, then quickly looked around for the ghost. Carleton was the only one in the room, sitting cross-legged on his bed and squeezing his red stuffed tyrannosaurus. "You're all wrinkled," he added.

I looked down at my sweatshirt and jeans. He was right—they made me look like a prune.

Feeling a lump near the end of the bed, I pulled the squashed green stegosaurus out from underneath the covers (how in the world did it get down there?), climbed out of bed, and stumbled toward the bathroom. I couldn't believe I hadn't woken up in time to run.

I could go out and run now, but I felt too exhausted. It was as if I'd lived a whole life in the night—someone else's life, in a farmhouse, with a sister who laughed. I didn't know where the snow and the cribbage boards and the card games fit into that life. I didn't even know whose life it was. Could the ghost haunt my dreams now?

There was no sign of the Hambricks when I got downstairs and the van had disappeared—maybe they all went to church. There was also no sign of Dad, and I didn't want to look for him. I was afraid I'd find out he'd gone with them. I made a fresh peanut butter and marmalade sandwich for breakfast and headed out onto the porch.

The ghost was standing in the backyard, floating just above the patch of poison ivy. "This yard needs tending if you expect to put in any crops," he said, his tone disapproving. "Is this what you meant when you said you needed help also?"

I dropped my sandwich and stumbled back inside, but the ghost was suddenly beside me in the hallway.

"Red—listen to me. I know you can hear me. I need to know about my family. You can understand that, can't you? All I need is a little help—then you can forget you ever saw me."

I understood—but how could I help him? I headed into the kitchen and was surprised to see Nicole at the refrigerator, pouring herself a glass of apple juice.

"What is this, return of the living dead?" she asked, looking me over as she sipped her juice.

A brisk breeze suddenly swirled around the wind chimes, setting the butterflies and hummingbirds pealing at full volume. Nicole almost dropped her glass.

"Make it stop!" she shouted.

I swiped my hand at the chimes, tangling them, then jerked the window down. The racket level dropped as if I'd hit the volume control on a remote.

I turned and saw tears in Nicole's eyes.

"So what's with all the wind chimes?" I asked, looking away.

She set the glass down and swiped at her eyes. "Mom . . . always liked them," she said softly. "She told me she liked the precision of the notes in the wind and the fun shapes the chimes come in. Daddy knew it, and he'd look for new chimes he thought would make her smile. We'd go together to flea markets or novelty stores, and he'd see something and show it to me. 'Do you think Mom would like this one?' he'd ask. Then he'd buy it for her."

Her voice quavered, and Nicole picked up the glass and took a long drink. "After he died, Mom and I were going through the things in his workshop, and we found all these boxes of chimes—more than a dozen—that he hadn't even given her yet. She sat down on a stool and cried. Then she hung the chimes up—everywhere. I hate them! I wouldn't let her hang any of them out on the porch, because that's my place to sit. But she's put them everywhere else."

She glanced at me, then quickly looked away. "Having them all up means he's never coming back," she said.

I didn't know how to tell her I knew just what she meant. I searched the entire house after Mom left, thinking she must have left something for me—an explanation, a birthday present for my tenth birthday. Something. I didn't see anything at all, so I thought she must be coming back right away.

I guess finding all those wind chimes made Mrs. Hambrick feel better. Maybe she knew how much her husband had loved her. He meant to stay around long enough to give each box of chimes to her. But it seemed to make Nicole feel worse. Even if he hadn't meant to leave, her father was lost for good.

But I didn't know how to say any of that, and Nicole just muttered, "It's freezing in here." She grabbed her glass and walked out of the kitchen.

"It's hard to lose someone you love," the ghost said quietly, and I jumped, not realizing he was still there. "I thought my heart would never mend from losing my mother. And when I realized my sister was gone, and everyone else in my family, I knew I could never rest until I found them."

We'd both lost the people we loved best in our families. If things had been different, maybe we could have been friends. But how could I be friends with a ghost soldier who had somehow dragged me through the window into his battle—and his death?

I tried to take a deep breath, but the icy air hurt my throat. "I'm really sorry about your sister and your mother, but I just can't help you. Please—can't you leave me alone?"

He didn't answer in words. There was just a whirl of cold air that wrapped itself around me.

It was a long afternoon. If I sat on the porch swing, the ghost sat above the railing and complained about the overgrown yard. If I sat indoors, the ghost set the nearest of the wind chimes tinkling like crazy. And I'd slept so long, I couldn't hide under the covers and escape from it all that way.

What if I really was supposed to help him? What if that was why I had come to North Carolina? And what if I failed? Maybe that's why Mom left me—because I was scared to try things.

Mom was always talking about new things she wanted to try, like flying an airplane. "Wouldn't it be wonderful to fly free up in the sky? Dipping and soaring all alone?" I thought it sounded exciting, but I liked hearing her talk about doing it more than I liked the idea of doing it myself. Mom would have welcomed the ghost. I felt ashamed to admit it, but I was scared of getting too close to that icy cold, scared of the minié balls whistling over my head and the bayonet flashing in the sun. I was scared of trying to help him, scared that I wouldn't be able to. I wished I wasn't special enough to see ghosts. But that didn't make him go away.

Mrs. Hambrick, Carleton, and Dad had gone to church. Dad never went to church at home. I felt kind of jealous that he'd gone with the Hambricks and hadn't taken me.

They had Sunday dinner in the middle of the afternoon, and Dad told me to help Nicole and Carleton set the dining room table. Nicole was spreading a lacy tablecloth over the large polished oak table when I got there.

"Here," Nicole told me. "Follow behind and put the glasses out. They're just everyday ones, so it won't matter if you drop one." She balanced a stack of dishes with delicate blue and gold patterns, and Carleton lugged an armload of silverware.

I followed Nicole, putting glasses out at the right-hand corner of each place setting she laid down, with Carleton behind me, carefully positioning the knives and forks and spoons.

The ghost stood at the end of the table, glaring at me. "You can't ignore me forever," he said, his voice fierce, as if he were warning me.

I stared at the table settings, wishing I wasn't afraid and could just exorcise him or something. Then he moved suddenly, swooping behind Carleton.

"Hey!" the kid cried, dropping the silverware with a clatter. "That's cold!"

The ghost stared at me, and I looked away, trying to ignore my shaking hand as I put a glass at the place Nicole had just set.

Darting suddenly, the ghost appeared on the far side of me, beside Nicole. She shrieked, and the last dishes crashed to the table.

"What is it?" Mrs. Hambrick cried, running into the dining room. "Nicole—how could you?"

The bottom plate was fine, but the top one was cracked. Nicole looked at it, shaking her head, her eyes wide. Beyond her, the ghost looked at me.

"I didn't do anything!" Nicole told her. "There was this gust of cold air and—and—the plates suddenly turned cold. I mean—they felt like they'd just come out of the freezer or something! My hands felt numb, and I guess I just couldn't hold the plates. I didn't mean to!" She looked at me sharply. "Maybe *he* did something. I never broke anything before!"

Mrs. Hambrick sighed. "Don't blame someone else to excuse yourself, Nicole."

"But—but—" Nicole spluttered. I just stood there holding the glasses. I couldn't tell them I was being haunted.

Who'd believe me? But I felt bad. In a way, I guess it was my fault she'd cracked the plate.

Suddenly, the ghost turned and headed for the window. The sets of wind chimes hanging there exploded into noise, and Mrs. Hambrick jumped.

"What's going on?" Dad asked, appearing in the doorway wearing oven mitts. "Why's it so cold in here?"

"I have no idea," Mrs. Hambrick said, unsteadily. "A freak wind, I suppose." She glanced at me uneasily, then went into the kitchen with Nicole. I just stood there clutching the glasses, waiting for the ghost to swoop over me.

He faced me, his black eyes pools of sadness. "I can't just go back to Fort Stedman and pretend I didn't find you. I've been waiting for so long that my life before seems nothing but a dream, and the waiting is the only thing real. I have to tell you my story—and you have to listen."

Part of me wanted to say okay, I'd do it. I'd thought seeing ghosts was wonderful, but having them need me to help them was frightening. I put down the last glasses and headed to the kitchen.

The ghost called after me. "I'll be waiting for you, Alexander."

Chapter Seven

WHEN RICHESON CAME MARCHING HOME

It was still light when I carried my recorder and sheet music out to the porch after we cleaned up from supper. It had been a slow meal, with lots of food I pushed around on my plate in between passing serving bowls. I could barely eat the country ham. It tasted salty and my mouth felt too dry. Dad and Mrs. Hambrick were talking about some computer company in a place called Research Triangle Park, and Carleton chattered away at Nicole. She was still steamed about the cracked plate, and I had to be extra careful myself, helping her load the dishwasher, because my hands were shaking. All I could think of was the ghost waiting for me.

I took my recorder so I'd have an excuse to go off alone, but I didn't need one. Dad and Mrs. Hambrick were sitting in the living room together, and nobody asked me where I was going. The smell of oranges drenched the porch when I stepped outside, and the ghost floated a little above the porch rail, as if he were sitting there. I wanted to tell him okay, I'd listen, but I couldn't frame the words.

I slid the pieces of my recorder together and tried to play a song by heart, a Shaker tune I liked, "Simple Gifts." The notes were meant to be played smoothly, but my breath came in jerks and the rhythm fell apart. I was scared of the ghost and ashamed of myself and angry, too—angry at Dad for bringing me here, and even angry at Mom, for once—angry at her for telling me I was special for seeing ghosts and then leaving me to face them alone. Too many feelings were mixed up inside of me. I needed a different kind of music. I thumbed through the music book, almost ripping the pages.

"Red, I'm sorry," the ghost said. "Are you upset because I frightened the girl? I truly did not mean for her to crack that plate. I wish I could apologize to her."

Well, he couldn't! But I wasn't going to answer him. I just clamped my lips over the recorder's mouthpiece and stared hard at the wavering notes on the page of music. It was a book of American folk music, and I saw the song was "Dixie." Its jazzy, syncopated lilt seemed better suited to the nervy way I was feeling, and I let the music break loose inside of me. I could feel my breathing even out as I phrased the notes, and the anger inside of me quieted.

When the last note hung in the air, I turned the page and saw "When Johnny Comes Marching Home." You never got home, I thought at the ghost, and felt unexpectedly sorry for him. My fingers rested on the recorder stops instead of gripping the instrument, and my breathing was steady as the melody rippled smoothly.

Then the music swelled. Not stopping, I looked up and saw the ghost blowing into a harmonica. His eyes smiled as he slid the stops up and down across his mouth, and he tapped the beat in the air with his right boot.

We blew the last note together and smiled at each other.

"Music sure has a way of settling folks down, doesn't it, Red?" he asked peaceably.

I slid the pieces of my recorder apart and wiped down the inside. I could go on running from the ghost, or I could face him and find out what he wanted. I looked up, and he was still smiling faintly at me. I took a deep breath, said, "I guess it does," and realized I'd decided to stop running away. "Okay—you'd better tell me how you think I can help you, Richeson." I shook my head. "That's quite a mouthful. Is that what everybody called you?"

He grinned. "Fewer syllables than Alexander, if you're counting. Richeson is a family name—my grandfather's name on my mother's side. My oldest brother, George, got my father's name. And the Francis comes from Francis Scott Key."

"You're related to Francis Scott Key?" I asked, impressed.

"Of course not," he said, wiping his harmonica. "A lot of families named their sons for heroes in the War of 1812— their middle names, at least. My friends called me Rich," he added, almost shyly.

I put the pieces of the recorder away in their case and leaned back on the porch swing. It's funny how you can get used to that smell of oranges and even the cold. "Okay, Rich," I told him, "tell me what you want."

"I need to know what happened to my family," he said. "It should be quite simple for an out-of-timer to find out, but I can't do it myself. I tried."

"How am I supposed to tell you what happened to your family?" I asked.

"You can hold things," he explained. "I can't."

I frowned. "But you can stand on the ground, and you can hear me and the others and see us."

"Being a ghost can be confusing," he said wryly. "I still have my senses—I can see and smell and hear and feel—I can feel tired, for instance, and I sleep when I do, or I can feel sore if my boots rub my feet, or feel the weight of my musket. I'm not standing on the ground, though—I'm just, well, sort of floating here. I could as easily be up in the sky, but it seems more polite to be here beside you. I could even taste if I could only eat! And sometimes I do feel hungry when I smell good food like that country ham tonight. But I can't hold food or anything else."

"What do you call that?" I asked, pointing to the harmonica.

He held it up, turning it so that the light from the living room reflected off the polished metal side plates. "But this is from my time, from my life. You'd have trouble holding it, I think."

As he crossed the porch and held it out to me, I reached out one finger tentatively. The little instrument felt like a slab of dry ice, so cold it burned, and my finger went numb immediately. I jerked the hand back and tucked my finger in my armpit to thaw out. "I see what you mean!"

He smiled sadly and slipped the harmonica into his knapsack. "I can't hold anything in your time, or in any time after my death. My hand just goes through it as if it's nothing but a cloud. And there's something I need to get that you can hold for me. I think that will tell me where my family went."

Rich sighed and propped his musket beside him. He floated cross-legged on top of the plank floor, leaning back against his bedroll. "We owned a farm in Wake County, North Carolina, near Stirrup Iron Creek."

"Two Stirrups," I said, remembering his words at the battlefield.

"That's right." He nodded. "My father called it that after the creek. The farm wasn't that big—only about seventy acres. My father and my older brothers, George and Jefferson, laid in a good crop of tobacco each year, as well as the vegetables for the family. I loved growing things even when I was younger, and I had ideas about how to improve the farm." Rich sat up straighter, pointing at the sloping yard beyond the porch as if he were still alive to make improvements. "I could see the mud in the runoff after the rain, and I got this idea that we should plow *around* the slope instead of up it. Father said he'd consider it after the War . . ." His voice trailed off and he looked sadly at the Hambricks' yard. "Doesn't it hurt you to see this tangle of weeds?"

I nodded and set the recorder down on the porch swing. "It's not my yard, but I've been aching to do some work on it. We don't live on a farm, but we've got a garden at home—my mother loves flowers." I went down the porch steps and crouched beside what looked like it had once been a flower bed. When I tugged at the tangle of ivy, it resisted for a moment, then began to tear free. I could see stunted dandelions and other weeds matted beneath the ivy and wondered what else was there. "Go on," I said as I worked. "Tell me about your family."

"There were five of us that survived," Rich said, kneeling down above the patchy grass beside me. "George was the oldest. He was seventeen in '59, before the war. Then there was Amalie. Avery came next, but he died of whooping cough before I was born. Jefferson was fourteen, then came Harriet—she took sick and lived just long enough to be christened. I was next, and then Louise. Mother lost one more boy, Andrew, and a girl, Marietta, before Hiram was born."

He pointed out a tendril of ivy that I'd missed, and I tugged until it ripped out. "Little Hiram lived only a few weeks, and then Mother died—a fever. That was 1859, right before I turned ten."

My hand jerked and the ivy slid through it. Mom had left just before I turned ten, also. "What is it?" Rich asked.

I looked back at the weeds. "I lost my mother when I was about the same age."

"Oh." He was silent for a moment. "I'm sorry, Alexander. I didn't realize your mother was gone."

I shook my head. "Not like that—she's not . . . dead. She left." I swallowed and began pulling the weeds the ivy had hidden. "I don't want to talk about it."

Rich nodded after a moment. "I miss my mother, but not the same way I miss my sister Louise." His voice cracked, and I remembered his envious tone when he'd asked if Nicole was my sister. "We were the youngest, and I suppose we were a bit spoiled. Louise had the most wonderful ideas for ways to get out of chores, and a whole collection of hiding places around the farm so we wouldn't get caught. Once we were free, she came up with terrific games that we could play. I would be Sir Lancelot in shining armor, and she would be Joan of Arc." He laughed. "Centuries apart, of course! But things like that never bothered Louise. At Petersburg, I thought about Louise all the time, wishing I were still back home. Things didn't work out at all the way I thought they would when I enlisted."

"Why did you enlist?" I asked, tugging at a tough dandelion with a deep root. "I mean—you can't be much older than I am. They wouldn't let *me* in the Army."

"I was fifteen," Rich said. I'd thought he was younger—he was shorter than me. But with his lean frame, just muscles and no fat, he also looked older than fifteen. "The Confederate

Army was desperate for soldiers. That Christmas, in 1864, Governor Vance made a speech calling on every man who could handle a musket or stand behind a breastwork to rally to the Confederacy's defense. And the summer before, President Davis said that the War would go on until the last man fell in battle, and his children seized his musket and fought on. George and Jefferson had joined the Army long before. I knew it was time for me to do my part.

"I didn't even tell Louise what I was planning. I was half afraid she'd beg me to stay and half afraid she'd insist on coming with me and we'd both be sent home. I just slipped out early and enlisted at the county courthouse." He smiled faintly. "They weren't worried about ages. The man just said, 'You look sixteen, Chamblee,' and I didn't disagree, so he gave me the oath right there and I was a soldier."

I ripped out the last of the weeds and sat back on my heels.

"Look," Rich said, pointing, a smile spreading all the way to his eyes.

I smoothed the soil around a squashed-looking crocus that was starting to straighten up now that the weeds were gone. "I bet there's more of them, but it's getting too dark to work tonight." Somehow twilight had closed in around us. I stood up, brushed off my jeans, and headed back to the porch swing. "I don't get it. If your brothers were already in the Army—"

"And my father was in the Home Guard," he interjected, following me.

"Then why did you have to join? Your family had already done its part."

"It was not merely a matter of doing your part!" Rich said sharply. "Friends in South Carolina wrote to us. Sherman's raiders—" His face darkened ominously, and I shivered a little. "I cannot call them soldiers," he went on, almost biting off the words, "for they dishonored the idea of patriotic duty! I faced Union soldiers at Fort Stedman—they were honest men who fought for what they believed, even if they were the enemy. But they fought against armed men, as soldiers should, not against women and children. Sherman's raiders beat on the door of a nearby house in the middle of the night and turned the women and children out into the dark!"

His fists clenched around his musket. "Children! They were children, not soldiers who could fight back!"

I nodded and thought that he didn't seem to realize he was just a kid himself, who shouldn't have had to fight soldiers.

"The raiders ran through the house," he went on, his voice strained, "setting torches to the curtains and bed quilts, screaming like banshees. My father's friend wrote that the crackling of the flames and the crashing of rafters were horrible. The people themselves were left destitute—the Yankees took everything, even the family jewelry. And these marauders were marching toward Two Stirrups! I wanted to stop them before they ever reached our county. I had to keep Louise safe."

I could understand that—he'd made up his mind to fight for his family the same way I'd made up my mind to fight for mine. We just had different ways of standing up for what we wanted. But you couldn't just sit and do nothing when your world was falling apart.

"I thought I'd be sent to face Sherman," he went on. "But they needed replacements in Petersburg the worst, so they sent me there."

"So that's how you got stuck in Petersburg with Lee's Army," I said.

"I couldn't believe I wasn't even going to fight in North Carolina! I almost deserted," he said, turning his musket around in his hands. "I'm ashamed to admit it, but if you're going to help me you deserve to know it all. One of the veterans who'd been with the 49th for a couple of years, Noah Langston, befriended me. I told him I had signed up to keep my family safe. It wasn't right that I was here while Sherman was getting closer every day to Louise and Amalie. I told Noah I had to go to them!"

He reached into a pouch at his belt, took out a cloth, and began wiping the barrel of his musket, as if he'd rather concentrate on that than think about what he was saying. "A lot of soldiers were deserting that winter, going home to their families. I told myself if the others were doing it, then it must be all right. Sometimes you tell yourself things like that when you know what you want to do is wrong but everything all around you seems wrong, too."

I nodded. I knew all about telling myself one thing, even when I knew it was wrong. But I couldn't admit that to anybody else the way Rich just came right out and told me.

"But Noah stopped me," Rich went on, and I quit thinking about myself and paid attention to him. "He didn't report me, or stand guard on me, or anything like that. He just gave me a piece of advice, and I've never forgotten it." The hand wiping down the musket paused, and he looked out into space as if he could see his friend in front of him. "Noah said, 'You do your job by holding your position here, Chamblee. If you stand fast and hold these earthworks, then you'll keep these civilians in Petersburg, and our government in Richmond, safe. And remember—there's some Virginian in General Johnston's Army who's standing fast against Sherman's raiders, in order to protect your people at Two Stirrups. You can best keep your sisters safe by standing here and doing your job, Chamblee, just as he's doing his. And I keep my wife and children safe by standing fast beside you.'"

Rich swallowed, and when he looked up at me, his dark eyes glittered as if they were damp. "So I stood fast. There wasn't much training, but Noah worked with me. My father had taught me to shoot straight and reload fast to shoot again when he took me hunting, and Noah taught me to keep shooting when someone was firing at me. He made me drill and drill until I could go through the steps of tearing open a paper cartridge, pouring in the powder, seating the minié ball, setting the percussion cap, aiming and firing—

almost without thinking about it. He showed me how to use my bayonet as a rest for my ramrod so that I could load even faster."

He went back to wiping down his musket, his hands moving methodically over every inch of it as though he had done the task thousands of times. I guess he must have. "Noah taught me everything he knew, and I stayed with the Army of Northern Virginia instead of going home to Two Stirrups. When General Gordon ordered us forward, I advanced with the 49th and we took Fort Stedman, and we stood fast even when the blue coats pushed our men back. We stood fast to cover the retreat. I stood fast with Noah and the other survivors from D Company, and after Noah fell, I stood fast while the Yankees overran Fort Stedman, and I died standing fast."

Rich had finished cleaning his musket, and he held it so tightly his long, thin fingers seemed to sink into the wood of the stock. "So I did my job, just like Noah told me, but when I died my last thought was of Louise, and I couldn't rest until I knew what had happened to her. I guess I must have drifted in some sort of limbo for a while, because I was still at Petersburg when I came back to myself, but the other Confederate soldiers were gone. There were only blue uniforms everywhere. So I went back to Two Stirrups to make sure Louise was safe."

"Like Odysseus coming home after the Trojan War," I said suddenly.

"That's right," Rich said, and smiled. "My father used to read the *Iliad* and the *Odyssey* at night, and George and Jefferson and I all dreamed of being brave as Achilles and coming home to everyone's surprise like Odysseus." Then his smile faded. "I sure didn't dream of coming home dead."

He looked away. "It took a long time walking, because I got tired, even if I was a ghost. And my bedroll and haversack straps still felt like they were rubbing my neck, even though I didn't exactly have a neck anymore. Sometimes I'd ride a ways in a passing wagon. I found out I could reach through things, but if I concentrated I could sort of rest on top of something, and a wagon went faster than I could walk." His voice grew quieter, and I had to lean forward to hear him. "The wagons had wounded men, going home, and sometimes they felt the cold—a couple of them even woke up and saw me if they were far enough gone from their wounds. If I didn't frighten them, I'd just ride along for a while. If they got upset, I'd slip off and keep walking. I knew I had to see Louise before I could rest and be certain that our soldiers had stood fast and kept Two Stirrups safe. But when I got there—" He shook his head as if he still couldn't believe it. "She was gone."

I straightened on the porch swing with a jerk, and the recorder case slid off and thumped to the plank floor. I guess I should have known she'd be gone, since he told me he needed my help to find out what happened to his family, but

I just wasn't expecting his sister to disappear. I asked, "You mean she left?"

"The whole family left," he said. "At least, whoever was alive. I don't know that either." He banged one fist against his cartridge box. "The fields were burned, the barn burned to the ground. Part of the house still stood, but it was only a scorched shell of charred walls, every pane of glass shattered before the fire went out. Inside I saw shreds of ripped and blackened upholstery hanging from broken furniture. The hardwood floors that Amalie used to make Louise work so hard to scrub were stained black with smoke." Rich shuddered. "Two Stirrups—a ruin."

"But they must have been somewhere nearby," I said, horrified. Then I wished I hadn't said anything as I finished the thought. "Unless they were . . . dead."

Rich shook his head. "I went to the other farms looking for Louise—but they were all in shambles, too. Then I searched farther and farther, listening to people talking, mostly Yankee soldiers and those Reconstructionists who took over running the county. No one ever said anything about the Chamblees."

"Then how can I find them?" I asked, overwhelmed by the hopelessness of the puzzle.

"After I searched," Rich said, sitting upright, "I realized that Louise would never have just gone without leaving word for me—at least, unless she really was dead. And I wouldn't believe that! So I checked our hiding place. Louise was the one who had first discovered it, of course." He smiled. "It was a hollow in an oak tree—an obvious choice, except that you really couldn't see it. There was a cluster of oaks growing too close to each other, and this one had low-hanging branches—they hid the hollow completely."

His smile faded. "I looked in the tree, and there was something tucked into the hollow. It was a metal box—enough sun came through the bare winter branches to make it sparkle silver."

"So what was it?" I demanded.

Rich shook his head in frustration. "I don't know! I reached inside, but my hand slid right through it. I couldn't hold it or open it—but who else could have known about the hollow? Amalie didn't, that's for sure. Louise used to snatch sweets from the kitchen when Amalie was baking, and she never once found where we stashed the treats. Louise would wrap them up to keep them fresh, and we'd eat them together the next day."

Then he leaned forward eagerly. "I've been pondering on it a long time, Alexander. If Sherman's raiders burned the farm, Amalie and Louise knew they'd have to go someplace safe, at least until Father came home, or George or Jefferson or I got back from the War. I think Louise left a note in the tree, telling me where she went. If I could only read it, I could go there and find out what happened to her."

I felt a sudden surge of envy. When Mom had gone, the only thing I found was her old soprano recorder, wedged in the back of an otherwise empty lilac-scented drawer. I told myself she'd left it especially for me and taught myself to play it, but there was no note or anything. Deep down inside, I was afraid she'd forgotten it, or just hadn't wanted it anymore. It didn't seem fair that the ghost's sister had cared enough to leave him something and Mom hadn't. "Rich," I said finally, "that was a long time ago. Even if she left you a note, the paper would have disintegrated outdoors."

He shook his head impatiently. "That's why she put it in the metal box—to keep it dry and safe. But I need you to take the box out of the tree and open it for me."

"But even if the note tells you where to go, she'll be long gone," I told him.

"I know that." He looked away from me, out into the shadowy yard. "But she'd have grown up and married. She'd have children, and they'd have children. If I only knew she got out safe, I'd know our family survived. And I guess I'd know it was worth it, standing fast at Fort Stedman."

I realized I was committed now. I wanted more than anything else to know it was worth it, standing fast for Mom, keeping everything ready for her. If Rich felt the same way, I had to help him. I reached down and picked up my recorder case. "All right," I said. "I don't know how to find Stirrup Iron Creek, but if we can get there, I'll take down that box and open it for you."

"Thank you, Alexander," he said, smiling. "I knew you would help me in the end. I knew there was a reason I saw you in the bomb proof. We're not too far from Stirrup Iron Creek right now."

Of course, I thought. It's not as if I'd find a ghost who needed help with a place way over in South Dakota. He's a North Carolina ghost—his secret hiding place would be right here. So it was no accident Dad had met Mrs. Hambrick and brought us to Durham after all. I didn't know why I had ended up with the job, but I was going to help this ghost, whether I liked it or not.

But I did wonder about something Rich hadn't mentioned; 1865 was a long time ago. Oak trees can live a long life, but would the tree still be there, protecting the metal box Louise had left?

Chapter Eight

FINDING STIRRUP
IRON CREEK

"How'd you like to come to Research Triangle Park with me?" Dad asked when I came in after my morning run. I had no idea what he was talking about. I'd been trying to figure out an excuse to look for whatever was left of Two Stirrups and the oak tree Rich had told me about.

Dad and Mrs. Hambrick stood over a map at the kitchen table. Dad looked strangled in a tie, and a sports jacket was hanging over the back of one of the kitchen chairs. I didn't know he'd brought nice clothes. Nicole sat on the far side of the table, eating a toasted bagel and staring off into the yard.

I jogged in place over by the sink to cool down, wondering why Dad was so dressed up. "What's in Research Triangle Park?"

Dad frowned at me, his eyebrows almost meeting in the middle of his forehead above his nose. It's the same exasperated expression he gets when he's rewritten a program ten times and it keeps crashing. "Weren't you listening at all last night? The software company we were discussing has its headquarters there. That area used to be farmland once, but it was all bought up for an industrial complex." His face relaxed and he grinned at me. "The Silicon Valley of the South."

"I thought Silicon Valley was in California," I said, concentrating on my cooldowns. "What's the big deal about this place?"

Dad glanced at Mrs. Hambrick. "They're interviewing me for a job, Alexander."

I stared at the tangled branches outside the kitchen, not wanting to hear about it.

"I told you that," Dad said quietly.

I knew he had. I just hadn't wanted to listen to him any more than I'd wanted to listen to Rich.

"I'm going upstairs to shower," I told them.

"When you come down, let me know if you want to go," Dad said. "If not, Nicole said she'd show you around."

Nicole practically choked on her bagel. Apparently I didn't fit into her spring break plans any better than she fit into mine.

"Where is this place?" I asked, edging closer to the table.

Dad pointed on the map. Sure enough, it was a big, pale green patch labeled Research Triangle Park. But it was shaped more like a jalapeño pepper than a triangle. Aside from the big streets that looked like parkways, there were only a few small streets running through it, with names like Intel Avenue and Laboratory Drive.

Then I saw it. A narrow blue line ran down along the east side of the green shape. The tiny words that curved alongside it read Stirrup Iron Creek.

A sudden cool breeze brought the wind chimes to life. "Sure, Dad," I said, watching the hummingbirds jostle. "I'll go."

Rich was waiting for me in the van, along with Dad and Mrs. Hambrick. I'd thought it would be just Dad and me. And the ghost, of course. Why did *she* have to come along?

"Paige set up the interview," Dad explained, as if he'd read my thoughts. He leaned around the front passenger seat as I climbed in. "After we're done, I thought we could go out to lunch—do a little sightseeing—whatever you'd like."

I knew Dad was trying to be friendly, but I didn't care about sightseeing in Durham, especially with Mrs. Hambrick. I wanted to take care of Rich's problem, then figure out how to talk Dad into going back home once and for all. Maybe he'd mess up the interview and they wouldn't want to hire him. That was something to hope for.

Rich grinned at me. "I knew you'd find a way to get us to Stirrup Iron Creek."

I checked to make sure that Mrs. Hambrick wasn't looking at me in the rearview mirror and grinned back at him in spite of feeling weird seeing him there and seeing Dad and Mrs. Hambrick just past him. Rich looked as solid and real as they did, and yet they couldn't see him. Or hear him. But they'd sure hear me if I tried to answer him.

I settled back to watch the trees go by and thought about going home to Indiana. I wondered if maybe Dad wanted to do something new—maybe he was sick of programming. Mom had always wanted to try new things, but I wanted things to stay the way they were—or at least the way they'd been. Maybe Dad was bored with our life in Indiana. The idea spooked me more than I would have thought. If he could get bored—would he get bored with me? Mrs. Hambrick turned onto a street called Cornwallis, and I saw a small green sign posted on the side telling us we were headed toward Research Triangle Park.

"Dad," I asked, "are you tired of writing programs?"

He looked surprised. "Of course not. I still love messing around with code, seeing what I can make computers do."

Mrs. Hambrick had to get into the conversation. "Did you know that 90 percent of programmers quit programming inside of five years, Alexander? Your father's in the 10 percent who seem to love it for life."

I wish she'd kept that little statistic to herself. What did she know about my dad, anyway? Did everybody quit one thing to try something new? Was Rich the only one who stood fast and stayed with what he was supposed to do? The road widened into four lanes, and we passed a cemetery and then some churches and a high school. I shifted uncomfortably in the van's seat. My back and shoulders felt stiff. "Why would they just quit programming, Dad?" I asked.

"I guess some of them get tired of trying to straighten out buggy code. And some of them probably get burned out with creating something new."

Rich listened to the conversation from the seat in front of me, but he didn't say anything.

The road had become more crowded, with buses chugging along and lots of cars pulling into parking spaces in front of the shops. I watched the traffic and thought about Dad's job interview.

"Is that why you're applying here?" I asked Dad finally. "Would you be doing something different than programming?"

Dad turned around in his seat and looked at me with his steady grey eyes. "No," he said. "It's a programming job, Alexander."

I felt the tension in my back and shoulders ease, and he smiled at me before he turned back around to face front.

At Research Triangle Park, wide green lawns stretched from the street down to new construction sites and up to low buildings with dark tinted windows, partly blocked from the road by perfectly trimmed hedges and saplings stuck in the ground at artistic intervals and held up with wires. The park looked polished and new and somehow artificial. I wondered what the farmland had looked like when Rich's family had lived there.

The ghost's face was drawn now, looking at the lawn as if he was seeing the burned fields after the war rather than the crops that grew here before he left home.

Mrs. Hambrick turned into a driveway. A big stop sign with a row of orange cones stood in the way. I could see a white one-story building beyond it, with those little wired trees blocking its windows. A security guard drove up in a black pickup truck, and I wondered how he got there so fast. When he climbed out and came over to the car, Mrs. Hambrick rolled down her window.

"Can I help you, ma'am?" he asked, looking across her at Dad, and then scanning the rest of the van. His eyes passed right through Rich, of course, but he frowned faintly at me.

"Yes, we've got a 9:30 appointment with Don Carey?" she said, almost as if she were asking him if that was all right. "Paige Hambrick and Bill Raskin."

The security guard shook his head. "You can't come in this way, Ms. Hambrick. You need to drive around the complex to get to the reception area. Take this road and turn left at the next traffic light. Then turn in at the second driveway."

He glanced once more at me, then added, "They'll call Mr. Carey for you from the guard shack."

"What is this place," I asked once we were out of the driveway, "a software company or some supersecret spy center?"

Dad laughed. "Software can be more supersecret than the spy business these days."

"I guess," I said. We drove by a driveway that led into some sort of park, with a little lake and picnic tables and basketball hoops, and then kept going past a hedge until we came to the traffic light and turned.

"There it is," Mrs. Hambrick said, pointing to a discreet sign that read Entrance.

As we pulled up to the guard shack in the middle of the drive, a door swung open and another security guard came out. At least this one was smiling.

"Can I help you folks?" he asked politely.

My dad leaned over. "Bill Raskin," he said, "and Paige Hambrick. We've got a 9:30 appointment with Mr. Carey."

"Let me call reception," the guard said. He went inside and spoke on a phone. A minute later he came back. "Please follow this driveway. You'll be met at the front door."

Sure enough, another guard was waiting for us in front of a white building with windows that reflected like mirrors. He pointed to a parking spot and Dad climbed out of the van.

"Mr. Raskin? Ms. Hambrick?" the guard asked. "Mr. Carey's expecting you." Then he looked at me, with a slight expression of concern on his face. "And this is?"

I slid the van door shut and wondered what the fuss was about.

"This is my son, Alexander," Dad said. "Is there a problem?"

The guard smiled again. "Mr. Carey is expecting you two, but not a youngster, I'm afraid. We have pretty tight security here."

Rich looked down and impatiently scuffed the air above the parking lot tarmac with one boot.

"That's all right," Mrs. Hambrick said quickly. "I'll just wait in the van with Alexander. You go on, Bill."

Dad got this worried look. Maybe he was counting on her for this interview. I guessed some teamwork was called for. Besides, I didn't exactly want to be stuck in the van with Mrs. Hambrick. I needed some time alone with Rich to find that tree. I turned to the guard and tried to sound very polite. "Look, sir, there's got to be someplace I can wait for them where you don't have to worry about security." I thought of that little park we'd driven past. "You know—someplace I could just sit under a tree or something?"

The guard's expression brightened. "We have a recreation area for employees and their families that's outside the secured area. I could let you wait there—if that's all right with you, Mr. Raskin?"

I gave Dad a smile, and he relaxed. "Sure. Thanks, Alexander."

"That was quick thinking," said Rich as the guard told the receptionist inside to call Mr. Carey to come meet Dad and Mrs. Hambrick.

I kept my mouth shut while the guard led me around the outside of the reception building, past another parking lot full of cars, and along another building in the complex. Then he opened a gate, and we turned a corner and started down a paved walkway to the park I'd seen. Close up, the place looked like some sort of fancy country club. I saw tennis courts and volleyball courts and basketball courts. The little lake lay beyond them, with a fountain in the middle. There were weeping willows and pine trees, with picnic tables in the shade beneath them.

"Wow," I said.

The guard laughed. "Think you'll be okay here, Alex?"

I didn't bother to correct him. "Yes, sir. I guess they'll come and get me when they're finished?"

He nodded, still grinning. "Or I will. Don't worry—we won't leave you here forever!"

I gave him a fake smile as he turned away. I was ready to bet they wouldn't leave anybody here and just forget about them. I mean—somebody might sneak into their supersecret buildings and make off with a prototype game or something.

"It should be over this way," said Rich, glaring at the departing guard.

"If we just take off, he'll follow us," I said. "Wait till he's out of sight."

"Why are they so worried about guests?" asked Rich. "Your father was invited—what has happened to our Southern hospitality?"

I walked across the grass toward the lake, keeping an eye on the guard. "This isn't a home, Rich," I told him. "They're not trying to be hospitable. It's a business—they design computer software, and it looks like they worry a lot about someone sneaking out with stolen programs."

"I saw this place change over the years," Rich said, frowning, "and realized it was no longer a home, but that's no excuse for such rudeness."

"You saw it change? But I thought you stayed at Fort Stedman."

"I would come back sometimes—" he said, "not often, perhaps every twenty or thirty years—to see if Louise, or someone with our family features, had ever come back to Two Stirrups. But I never saw anyone, so I'd return to the battlefield." He looked down like he was embarrassed. "It was lonely here with everyone gone. And there were other ghosts at Fort Stedman who couldn't rest either. We stayed together all those years. It's fairly quiet except on the anniversary of the battle. Then we all experience it again. I guess we always will."

"I wonder why you were the only one to realize I was an out-of-timer," I said, remembering all the soldiers crowded into Fort Stedman. Why had he zeroed in on me, someone who had lost his mother at the same age and who was going to end up so near Stirrup Iron Creek? There seemed to be an awful lot of coincidences bringing us together.

Rich looked at me. "When the right out-of-timer comes for one of us, he knows. It's meant to happen." He seemed to be taking it all in stride.

Rich glanced back at the computer company's buildings. "The last time I came here, I saw those buildings and the lake and these trees around us. The buildings were brand new and I went inside, just to see if I could recognize anyone—"

"Wait a minute," I said. "How did you get inside with all this security?"

He smiled. "They never saw me, of course. I walked through that first building, and there were lots of small rooms, with people sitting by themselves, pushing buttons and staring at lighted windows. Then I walked through another building, and I saw people wearing strange, thick spectacles, working with tiny strips of gold and copper, laying them down in patterns on shiny green plates of something—glass or metal perhaps? I watched them for a long time but couldn't understand the purpose of their work."

"Those green plates are called circuit boards," I tried to explain. "They make a computer work. The guys in the little rooms were working at computers."

"Computers? Yes—that was the word they used," said Rich. "But what does a computer do?"

I scratched my head. I used my Mac for everything from games to writing papers to doing my math homework. Big companies used their computers to figure payroll and calculate engineering statistics and utilities usage, I guessed. "Well," I said slowly, "basically it calculates things, only it does it really fast. And it remembers the calculations forever—at least until you tell it to forget them."

"It figures?" Rich asked. His eyes widened. "Instead of working out the mathematics on paper, or trying to calculate it in your head, this computer figures?"

"Basically." I wondered how something so simple as turning on my Mac could be so complicated when you tried to explain it.

Rich turned around and looked back at the buildings with awe. "They make these circuit boards and computers right here?"

I nodded.

A grin lit up Rich's face. "And the Yankees said the South would never have industry! They said we couldn't build anything here—we could only grow things and we'd never amount to much. Hah! And now the Yankees are buying *our* circuit boards! At Petersburg we tried to figure the angle and corrections to aim the mortars, and we had to do it all with pencil and paper—half the time we got it wrong. To have a computer that could figure for you! And we're building them right here in North Carolina!"

He let loose a whoop of delight and I laughed with him. Then I remembered where we were and hoped the guard wasn't watching. He'd think I was crazy, laughing all alone in the park. "How about we find this box that Louise left for you?"

Rich looked around suddenly. "They've cleared the land," he said, his face stricken as if the thought had only just occurred to him.

I studied the trees around us. "Some of the pine trees are old," I told him. "Where's your oak tree? If these trees lasted, it could have, too."

He looked at the pines. "They *are* old," he said slowly, "much older than the computer buildings. Our house was back there, near where the buildings are, but the oak was over that way from the house, near the creek." He pointed his musket past the pines and weeping willows, to the far edge of the recreation area. "Come on."

I followed Rich, ducking beneath the weeping willows and sweeping aside their drooping branches while he appeared to walk right through them. The sight was kind of creepy. We crossed the street we'd driven up before, then walked along a lawn and went over the paved top of a culvert filled with swampy, stagnant water.

"There." Rich pointed to a stand of scrub oaks and pine trees. "It should be around there, just this side of the creek."

"That's Stirrup Iron Creek?" I asked, looking down at the murky water, thick with overgrown weeds.

"Well, the creek used to be much larger," he said. "But they changed its course as they cleared the land." He shook his head in amazement. "I saw this powerful machine pushing the dirt—no horses at all, just this big machine! To change the course of a waterway with an axe and a shovel and a mattock is a tremendous undertaking, but that machine made it so easy."

"I don't know—it seems a waste to sacrifice the creek and change the lay of the land in exchange for industrial development," I told him. "I'd hate it if someone dug up my garden back home to widen a street or build another house or something."

Rich looked at me, his black eyes unreadable. "I suppose you have to choose whether to move forward or stay where you are. You can grow things on the land, or you can build industry, even if it changes the land. We might have won the War if we had built more industry back then."

I shrugged and followed Rich toward the trees.

But when we got there, there was no sign of his tree with the low-hanging branches. I couldn't see any old oak trees at all, just some young pin oaks and scrub pines. And beyond those, I could hear a bulldozer digging—that must have been the machine Rich had seen before.

"The tree *must* be here!" Rich cried, frantically. "It was here the last time I looked!"

"When was that?" I asked. "The time you went through the buildings?"

He shook his head. "I—I don't think so. I believe I was pondering those green plates and didn't come over here to check. I could see other trees still standing. I just assumed . . ." His voice trailed off in a tired sigh.

"Well, it's gone now," I said. "Even if the tree *was* there that time, there wasn't anything you could have done about it, not unless you had someone to take the box out for you."

He jerked around suddenly and looked at me. "If the tree's gone," he said, "then someone must have found Louise's metal box and opened it!"

Maybe someone had, I thought. But how in the world could we ever find out what they did with it?

Chapter Nine

A New Plan

I led the way back to the recreation area slowly, knowing how heartsick Richeson must feel.

"What if someone took it and kept it?" he demanded, pacing angrily right through the weeping willow branches. I closed my eyes and tried not to watch. No wonder he couldn't take Louise's box, the way he just passed through things like that. It made me feel queasy. "I'll never find it then!"

He turned to face me, his eyes blazing. "There has to be some record of them—there *has* to be!"

I sat on top of one of the picnic tables with my feet propped up on the bench, and wished I knew what to tell him. Finally I said, "I don't know what records we need to look at, and I probably couldn't find them even if I did know." I shook my head. "I don't know how to find your family, Rich. I can't even seem to keep my own family together. Maybe I'm just not strong enough—or brave enough." I took a deep breath. "You should have chosen a different out-of-timer."

He stopped pacing and looked at me silently for a few long moments. "You were brave enough to withstand Fort Stedman, Alexander," he finally said. "Anyway, it was not a choice—you were the one who was meant to help me." He came to the picnic table and sat beside me, his coolness wafting over as if I'd opened a refrigerator door. "Did you ever think that perhaps your mother's leaving had nothing to do with you? My mother didn't choose to leave me."

"Your mother died," I said, impatiently wiping my face. "It's not the same thing!"

"Louise didn't choose to leave me, either," he said evenly. "Yet she left. Your mother left for her own reasons, not because of you."

"Then why didn't she take me with her?" I whispered.

He shook his head. "I don't know." He thumped the butt of his musket helplessly on the air above the bench. "I wish I had answers for you, Red. But—" He paused. "I think there's a difference between your mother leaving and what happened to my family."

I knew he was right, and I knew I didn't want to hear it. "Yeah," I told him. "In your family, you're the one who left. And they waited for you as long as they could. But when you got back, they were gone . . . and now you've lost them."

"I haven't lost them forever," Rich whispered. "I'll find them."

I looked down at the table's surface and traced a pair of carved initials. "Well, I haven't lost Mom forever, either."

After a moment, Rich said, "If I could help you find her, I would."

I knew he meant it. And I wanted to help him, too. I just didn't have any idea how to begin. Then I remembered what Dr. Seagraves had said about searching for her family. Tentatively, I said, "Maybe we should try some sort of county records or the Genealogical Society or something."

Rich straightened up, his pale face brightening. "The county courthouse would have records of when the Yankee Reconstructionists seized the farm, and there'd be postal records, too. I wrote Louise the day before we attacked Fort Stedman. The Confederate postal service was still working, but mail could take a few weeks. If the letter didn't arrive before she left, they must have sent it on."

He added, "Someone from the regiment would have written to my family—if they weren't there to receive it, the letter must have gone somewhere."

But where? I shook my head helplessly, gripping the splintery edge of the picnic table.

"Hey, Alex?"

I jerked around and saw the guard waving at me from the corner of the building. I didn't think he'd been there long enough to hear me talking to the ghost, but I wasn't sure. I climbed down from the tabletop and started over to him.

"Your folks are just about finished," he said, leading the way back to the front reception building. "I thought you'd disappeared!" He chuckled, but it didn't sound too lighthearted. "I looked out to see if you were okay, and I couldn't find you."

Had he come over while we were at the creek? I wondered in alarm. Then I told myself, so what if he did? It wasn't illegal to take a walk. "I was just on the other side of the lake, sir," I said. "Exploring."

"Yeah? What did you see?"

I looked at him steadily. "Some trees and grass and a little creek that's dying. Anyway, what's wrong with my walking around?"

His eyes narrowed, but he kept his voice friendly. "Nothing at all, Alex, as long as you stay outside the secure area. It's just the labs and the plant we keep an eye on."

Yeah, right, I thought, but didn't say anything. These security guys kept their eyes on everything. I figured they liked it—maybe it made them feel important. "Well, you don't have to worry," I said, joking a little to see if I could loosen him up. "Dad's the computer whiz in the family, not me."

He shook his head. "What is it with kids, always deciding whatever their parents like isn't good enough? I'm a football fan—played in high school, too. So what does my kid decide to take up? Soccer! If I'd played soccer, he'd probably be in a football uniform today."

I gave him a half smile.

"Alexander, hi!" Dad called. As we got closer, I saw he was frowning. His eyebrows almost met in the middle of his forehead again. Maybe the interview hadn't gone too well.

"I'm sorry," he said as the guard headed back to the building. "I know I promised you lunch, but it turns out Don—the guy who's interviewing me—wants to talk a while longer, then take us out to lunch and show us around the plant this afternoon."

"No kids, in other words."

Dad looked embarrassed now, instead of frustrated. "Well, yeah."

"But *she's* going with you," I pointed out, rubbing it in.

"Come on, Alexander—Paige set this whole thing up!"

"Right. Whatever," I said, sighing. "So I'm supposed to hang out in the willow trees until you guys get back?"

He looked confused. "The recreational area?" I reminded him, waving my hand in the general direction of the place.

Dad looked relieved. "Oh. Well, Don said the guard could take you to the bus center and you could head straight back to Duke."

I thought about spending a boring afternoon at the Hambricks' house while Dad and Mrs. Hambrick were being lunched and fussed over. "Hey, what about lunch? And sightseeing?"

He glanced over his shoulder at the closed building. "We can sightsee tomorrow. I need a little support here."

I sighed. "How about I take the bus into downtown Durham, grab a burger, and do a little sightseeing on my own? I won't get into any trouble."

"Nicole said she'd be glad to show you around—" Dad began.

"You mean Mrs. Hambrick *told* Nicole to show me around if I didn't want to come with you guys," I reminded him. "Come on, Dad—you let me spend the afternoon in Indianapolis alone all the time."

"But this is a different city," he objected.

"So? It's not that big, and there probably aren't very many sights to see anyway. Nothing's going to happen to me. And it's better than sitting around here all afternoon, or getting stuck with Nicole."

He tried unsuccessfully to hide a smile. "Well, you're sure you'll be okay?"

I shrugged. "I guess."

Dad dug out his wallet. "Here's some cash, and some singles for the bus. Remember, Dr. Seagraves is coming over for supper, so don't be late."

Dad turned and waved at the building, and a minute later the guard showed up, driving a black pickup that looked exactly like the one that stopped us earlier that morning. I wondered if the company had a fleet of them.

Dad opened the passenger door and I climbed in, followed by Rich, who didn't seem to mind when Dad shut the door halfway through him. "He'll take you to the bus center, okay?"

Dad still looked kind of concerned behind his smile, so I took pity on him and gave him a little wave. "See you later!" I called.

He waved back, and the guard drove away. "In the mornings," he explained, "when people are coming to work, and in the evenings when they're going home, there's a shuttle that circles through the Research Triangle to and from the bus center. But it doesn't run during the day."

"Thanks for driving me," I said.

"No problem." He smiled at me. "It's easier than trying to keep an eye on a kid who likes to explore."

I had the feeling he was sure I'd been up to something, and I was relieved it took only a couple of minutes to get to the bus center. He pulled the truck up beside the curb and told me, "You can find a map inside, Alex. Look for the Redline route—that takes you back to Durham. The bus should be leaving in the next ten minutes."

I nodded and climbed out with Rich. "Thanks again."

The guard revved the engine and waved, and I headed inside, then looked around for that map. I had an idea. The map clearly showed the Redline bus running into downtown and then up to Duke University, just a couple of blocks from the Hambricks' house. But the bus stopped at other places in Durham, too. "Rich, where's this county courthouse of yours?"

He smiled at me, and for once his black eyes seemed to shine.

Then he peered at the map. He ran his finger along the roads, but he was looking southeast, away from Durham.

"No," I said, pointing at the map. "Durham's that way."

"I know. But Durham is in a different county. It didn't even exist when I was alive—there was just Orange County and Wake County here. Anyway, the Wake County court-house is in Raleigh."

I groaned. Dad would be furious if he found out I'd gone to Raleigh when I told him I'd stay in Durham. Then I saw that the same Redline route that came to the bus center from Duke University left the center five minutes later, going straight to Moore Square in downtown Raleigh—just a few blocks from the street mall marked on the map, and the courthouse Rich was pointing to. And it would only take two dollars and forty minutes to get there.

I was the one who suggested the whole thing, after all. And if I could help Rich, at least for once I'd feel like I'd been brave enough to do what Mom would have done. It was less than a five-minute wait for the next bus—just long enough to make me wonder how I'd find those records he was searching for. Then I stopped wondering and boarded the 10:45 bus headed to Raleigh instead of the one headed back to Durham and fed two dollar bills through the elec-tronic fare box.

Although the seat next to me was empty, no one sat down in it. I guess they could sense the cold, even if they couldn't see the Confederate ghost perched awkwardly above the molded plastic seat, holding his musket and looking at me like I was some kind of hero.

Chapter Ten

SURPRISES IN RALEIGH

I barely saw anything during the drive. Rich was as bad as Carleton—he wouldn't shut up.

"It was quite a walk to get to the Wake County courthouse, I tell you! There were no buses like these." He eyed the hard plastic seat appreciatively. "And every step I took, I kept worrying that they would send me home. I knew I was old enough to fight. Some things you just know; I could imagine a Yank soldier coming after Louise, and I knew I'd fight him—even kill him if I had to—to keep her safe." Rich looked serious as he said that.

"I thought of Louise at Fort Stedman, there at the end. I remembered what Noah told me, and I imagined she was there at Two Stirrups and the Yankees were coming. I thought about some Virginia soldier standing in front of her, holding back Sherman's raiders, and it was as if I were there in his place, not in Fort Stedman at all. I was fighting for my family."

He was silent for a few minutes, and I watched the state fairgrounds pass by the window. Then he said, "It must sound like I always thought about looking after Louise as though it were a life-and-death matter." He laughed a little. "We were just close. Amalie was close to George in the same way. I suppose that's why Amalie never got too angry with me and Louise when we hid instead of doing our chores when we were small, or slipped into the kitchen for extra treats. Sometimes I'd catch Amalie looking at the two of us with tears in her eyes after George enlisted—he signed up right after Fort Sumter in April of '61. But she would never admit how much she missed him."

He smiled a little. "You must be fair sick of hearing so much about these people you don't even know."

I shrugged. No one seemed to be paying attention to anyone else on the bus, so I muttered, "I kind of feel I do know them a little. What did Louise look like?"

His smile broadened. "Oh, she was beautiful! She had black hair, like me, but it was long and curly. It always got in her way so she kept threatening to cut it off. She said it wasn't fair that girls couldn't cut their hair short like boys. Her eyes flashed when she got mad—they were black like mine. When we were little, Mother used to dress us the same, and strangers thought we were twins." He sighed. "Father had blue eyes, and George and Amalie inherited them. When she was small, Louise used to cry because she didn't have Father's eyes. After Mother died, she didn't complain about it as much. I think our black eyes were something of Mother's to hold on to. And she didn't want to look like Amalie, after all!"

I grinned as we passed a sign announcing North Carolina State University. I tried to picture my mother—her black eyes, like mine, laughing. . . . Her long dark hair, loose and flowing across her back. Her hair was curly, too, wasn't it?

I suddenly realized I wasn't sure. I just couldn't bring her into focus—it had been too long since I'd seen her.

I shut my eyes and briefly saw her standing outside. She was looking down at the ground, and her hair hung limply. Her face was sad, and her whole body drooped.

I opened my eyes quickly. I didn't want to think of her like that. She only looked that way just before she left. I liked to think of her laughing and spinning in the garden. She'd turn round and round—I'd spin with her and get so dizzy I'd collapse in the grass. Above me, she'd just go on spinning and spinning.

I realized we were driving down city streets and had been for some time. "Is this Raleigh?" Rich asked, dubious. "I don't remember anything like this."

I said in a low voice, "It's a city—it's changed a lot. I'm sure everything's changed, like the creek did."

Rich shook his head. "Just as long as the courthouse is the same."

It wasn't.

We stood looking up at it. The map at the bus stop said the Wake County courthouse was at this address, and the sign on the building said this was the courthouse, but Rich insisted it didn't look anything like the building he remembered. I had to agree—this building looked really modern. It fronted on a walking mall that used to be the main street downtown, but the street was closed to traffic now. Long stone benches and small trees covered the mall. It was almost lunchtime, and lots of people were sitting on the benches, eating and reading newspapers.

"This isn't where I enlisted," Rich said flatly.

"Well, it's the county courthouse," I told him. "We've come this far—we might as well see if they've got the records here."

I climbed the steps to the entrance, walked past benches arranged around some planters filled with red and yellow tulips, and opened the door.

Inside, men and women wearing business suits headed down polished hallways, and a couple of police officers stood talking to each other in a corner. I saw an information desk and went over to it. The thin woman sitting there behind steel-rimmed bifocals didn't look too pleased to see me.

"What do you want?" She poked at her tight grey bun impatiently with a mechanical pencil. "You shouldn't be in here."

"I'm sorry," I stammered. "I was looking for the county courthouse, but this isn't the original courthouse, is it?"

She raised her eyebrows and her glasses slid down her nose. "Do you mean the original courthouse as in the colonial courthouse?"

I felt a flush burning up my neck. "No, ma'am. I meant the one from the—" Before I said "Civil War," I remembered the argument between Dr. Seagraves and Dr. Knox, and finished, "—the War Between the States."

The woman relaxed her eyebrows and smiled at me. "Well, as it happens, that building was finally torn down." Beside me, Rich groaned. "This courthouse was built in the seventies."

I sighed. "Oh."

"Why did you want to see the War Between the States courthouse?" she asked, taking her glasses off and letting them hang on a chain around her neck.

I realized I should have thought up a story before. "I was looking for some county records—for a school project."

She was already nodding. "Well, then that's not a problem. But you don't want the courthouse, young man. You want the State Library Archives on Jones Street. They've got original documents and microfilm records from every county, all the way back to when we were a colony."

I breathed a sigh of relief and let her show me where the library building was on a map, only a couple of blocks away.

"Just go upstairs to the Search Room," she told me. "They'll help you there."

"That was quick thinking, Red," Rich said as we crossed the mall. "Now we'll find out."

My stomach growled. "First I've got to get some lunch." I stopped at one of the mall vendors and bought a hot dog and a soft drink and sat on a bench to eat.

"Hurry up," Rich said impatiently.

"Go on," I told him around a mouthful of mustard and sauerkraut. "You know where it is—go check the place out while I finish."

Rich shook his head. "So many out-of-timers here—I might lose you."

I glanced at him standing there in his worn uniform with his musket and bedroll. "Well, I don't think I could lose you—you kind of stand out in a crowd."

He didn't smile, and I thought maybe he'd waited so long to find someone who could see him that he really was afraid of losing me. I swallowed the sauerkraut and shook my head. "Don't worry. I won't disappear on you. But let me eat, okay? And I've got to think up a good story for the people at the Archives. I need to make that school project more specific."

Rich looked a little confused, but relieved by my promise not to disappear. He sat down beside me, bringing his familiar chill along with him. Across the mall, people were sitting in shirtsleeves, fanning themselves with magazines and newspapers, and here I was with my own private air conditioner.

As I finished my hot dog, I worked out the details of what I was going to say. Then I pitched the wrappings and the can into a nearby trash bin and started off down the mall. "Let's go find those records."

I had no problem finding the State Library. I *did* have a problem, however, with the sign on the Search Room that said it was closed Mondays.

"I can't believe it! *One* day out of the week it has to be closed, and we pick that day!"

"Could we come back tomorrow?" Rich asked. He was already peering into the room, certain that the answers he was looking for were inside its locked files.

"I don't know if I can get away from Dad again," I told him. After messing up our lunch today, I was afraid Dad might make a big deal about spending time with me tomorrow. "Why don't you just—slip through, or whatever you do, and check the place out?"

Rich sighed, but he moved to the closed door. Maybe he'd see something from inside that could help us, like a door I could sneak in through.

"Hey, Rich—can you hear me?"

"Yes."

"Well, look around and see if there's a back door."

I stood in the hall, staring at the card catalog drawers on the other side of the locked door, wishing there were some way I could get inside to flip through them. It was all I could do not to kick the door, like a little kid throwing a tantrum. I wasn't so great at research, according to my teachers anyway, but if I could get in there with Rich, at least I could open drawers and things and he could tell me what to look for.

"What are you doing?" a voice behind me called out.

I thought fast. I didn't think I'd said anything for a couple of minutes, so hopefully the person hadn't heard me talking to Rich. I slowly turned around.

Chapter Eleven

THE ARCHIVES

Just down the hall a little ways, a plump black man in shirt-sleeves, with a tie dangling loosely around his neck, stood beside an open door, a potato chip in one hand.

"The Search Room is closed today," he said, then popped the chip into his mouth.

Maybe the Search Room was closed, but his door was open. If the rooms all connected along a back hallway the way the school offices did, then maybe I could figure out some way to get this guy out of his room and I could slip in the back. I walked toward him, my mind racing.

"Yeah," I said, "I can't believe it's closed! The lady at the courthouse sent me here, just twenty minutes ago. She never said anything about the Archives being closed on Mondays!"

"Well, the Archives are always open to the research staff," he explained, leading the way into a room marked "Non-Textual Materials Unit." At least he didn't just tell me to get lost. A suit jacket hung over the back of a desk chair, and he picked up another potato chip from a bag sitting beside a half-eaten sandwich on the desk. As an afterthought, he offered me the bag, and I took one to be friendly. "It's just the Search Room itself that's closed today—where the public can request archival documents."

He sounded very precise, like he knew all about the Archives. I read his name tag: Jesse Temple, Assistant Archivist. Then I came up with a better idea than getting him out of the way. I looked around. "So what's Non-Textual Materials, anyway?"

Jesse Temple lit up. "This is where we keep photographs, original prints, postcards, posters—things like that." He grabbed his sandwich, took a bite, and then swept it in a gesture to embrace the room around him. Sure enough, I saw another door in the back, and one on the side as well. Maybe that led directly to the Archives? He was saying, "We've got more than a million black-and-white photographs. That's before you count videotapes, sound recordings, and motion picture films."

"So this is all pictures—images and stuff?" I asked. "You don't do anything with stuff that's in writing?"

He took another bite of his sandwich and shook his head, and I thought my great plan wouldn't work after all. But then he surprised me. "What do you think—you can make sense out of pictures without any words? Sure we use the text archives—all the time! We just separate out the rooms this way so people who want us to do research for documents or pictures know where to go."

Bingo. Now let's see if my story would work. "So then, Mr. Temple—"

"Hey, call me Jesse." He grinned and held out his potato chip bag again.

"Thanks, Jesse." I smiled at him and took another chip. "I'm Alexander, from Indiana."

"All the way from Indiana? Just to do research here?" He looked delighted.

"Yeah, and that's the thing, see? I'm only here for a couple of days. But I'm missing some school, and the principal wasn't happy about that, until my dad promised I'd see some battlefields and historical places—we went to Petersburg on Saturday. My history teacher gave me this assignment. My dad's in meetings today, and I'm supposed to get this research done—I'll get into trouble if I don't have it."

"Well," Jesse said slowly, "what were you supposed to research?"

I swallowed the rest of the potato chip. "My teacher assigned me this family that lived in Wake County during the War Between the States. I'm supposed to find out who survived, what happened to them, and whatever else I can learn, I guess."

Jesse nodded. "Sure. They do that in the Archives Search Room all the time. People are always looking for their ancestors, you know? Look—I'm not supposed to do this for the public, but everybody else is off at lunch. If you tell me the family name, I'll see what I can find out."

I wished I could get him a whole case of potato chips! "It's Chamblee. They lived on Stirrup Iron Creek."

Jesse grabbed a pad and pen and began to take notes.

"Head of household? Or do you know?"

"Uh, the father's name was George," I told him. "There were five children—well, grown-up children, and teenagers. George and Amalie were the oldest, then there was Jefferson, and Richeson and Louise were the youngest."

Jesse nodded. "In the 1860s, right? Okay—you hold the fort here while I look in the back." He disappeared with his pad and sandwich, leaving his bag of chips behind.

I couldn't believe my luck—an Assistant Archivist with a soft spot for kids! I sat down on top of his desk, swinging my legs, and helped myself to a handful of his chips, hoping that no one would come in and wonder what I was doing there. This kind of research really worked, just like Dr. Seagraves said it would. If I could only find out Mom's maiden name for certain, I could do the same thing with her. Could it really be Thomson? There must be some clues at home. I'd go through the attic when we got back, and I'd figure out what county to start with and what questions to ask. For now, I only hoped Jesse wouldn't sense Rich in the room with him, trying to read the documents over his shoulder. And what if the records didn't have any of the answers Rich was looking for? Too many things to worry about.

And too much time going by—I took another handful of potato chips. Listening to them crunch was better than listening for footsteps in the hallway. But when Jesse came back in, he was holding a piece of paper with some notes on it and smiling. Unfortunately, Rich, who was right behind him, was frowning.

"Okay—I've got good news and I've got bad news. First of all, a land deed was filed for a seventy-acre piece of land owned by George Chamblee right on Stirrup Iron Creek, and the Chamblees are shown in the 1860 Census and on the tax lists through 1865." He shook his head. "But there's no mention of any of them in the 1870 Census, I'm afraid. I checked the Estate Records, and they don't show anything for the family."

"What does that mean?" I asked.

"Well, if the estate was passed on to someone, it would show up in the Estate Records," Jesse explained. I must have still looked blank, so he added, reluctantly, "If you die without a will, that's how they process your estate."

"Father must have died in the War," Rich said bleakly. "But why didn't George or Jefferson inherit the farm?"

"Oh," I said, wishing I could show him some sympathy. "So—what happened to the rest of the family?" I asked Jesse.

"Well, I also took a quick look through the land deeds between 1865 and 1870 to see what happened to the farm. The land was bought in 1868 by a Samuel Wheeler. He bought it from the state because they'd seized it for non-payment of taxes." Rich stiffened as Jesse shook his head. "That happened to too many people during Reconstruction.

The carpetbaggers from up north came down and set the taxes so high that a lot of North Carolina farmers couldn't pay to keep their own land."

He set the piece of paper down and looked at me. "I guess that's what happened to your Chamblees, Alexander."

"But that doesn't tell us anything!" Rich cried.

"Where did they go?" I asked Jesse.

"Some people looked for family if they had any in states that didn't secede. Some people went west. It would be hard to find someone unless you had an idea of where they'd gone."

I nodded. "What about," I asked hesitantly, "if they died?"

Jesse sighed. He opened a desk drawer and pulled out a bag of caramels. He offered them to me, but I shook my head, and he took one out and unwrapped it. "That's a tough one, actually. If a soldier died during the War, we have good records, because the Confederate government was meticulous about casualty lists. But by the middle of 1865, records get pretty haphazard."

I suddenly sat upright. "What about marriages?" Rich looked at me in surprise.

Jesse shook his head and popped the caramel in his mouth. "Wouldn't help," he said indistinctly, around the candy. "Same name we already checked."

"No—the girls, Amalie and Louise! What if they got married? Wouldn't the family be under their husbands' names in the Census?"

"But Louise was too young," Rich objected.

Jesse's eyes widened. Then he swallowed the caramel. "And so would the land and the tax records and everything! Good thinking—let me go check it out."

I waited until Jesse had disappeared back into the Archives. "When you left, maybe," I told Rich, "but not in a few years. And Amalie was old enough."

Rich looked unconvinced.

"Well, it's better than finding out they both died," I told him flatly. "I'm doing the best I can here—can you think of anything else we can ask him to look up?"

Rich shook his head and looked discouraged.

So did Jesse when he came back. "Nothing. And the frustrating thing is that it doesn't tell us much. You didn't have to get a license to get married before 1868, so it's hard to trace them. I checked the Marriage Bonds and the Record of Marriages, but there wasn't anything there. If there had been, we'd know for certain that one of the girls got married. Since there's nothing, we can't be sure."

"Great," I said, ready to give up.

"Hey—maybe this is what your teacher wanted you to find out," Jesse said. "You know—how hard it is to do research and how frustrating it can be."

If the assignment really had come from a teacher, that was probably exactly what she'd want me to find out. But not in this case. I slid off his desk. "I guess. Well, thanks for trying."

Then I remembered the metal box. "Say, Jesse—where does all this stuff come from? Not the county records, but all the pictures and stuff you've got here?"

"All sorts of places," he said, unwrapping another caramel. He looked pleased to change the subject.

Rich looked impatient. "Come on, Alexander. There's nothing here."

Jesse went on, "Private collections, or people find things and donate them."

"What about things other than pictures?" I asked, ignoring Rich. "What about things people might have hidden during the war?"

"You mean like jewelry, or family silver, and nobody came back to claim it?"

"Yeah, stuff like that. When I was at Research Triangle Park, I saw a lot of construction going on. Suppose they turn up something while they're digging, or tearing down the trees or something?"

Rich's eyes widened.

"Sure, 'at happens all 'e 'ime," Jesse said, chomping on the caramel. He opened a different drawer, and took out several sheets of paper clipped together. Then he swallowed. "If they bring it to the State Historical and Preservation people, then it gets studied and either goes into storage or out on display. You can see a lot of artifacts that people have found at the State Museum of History." He pointed it out on the top sheet of paper. "But sometimes the people who find artifacts give them or sell them to a private collector. Some of those objects come to the state eventually, but many of them are displayed in private museums. There are lots of them in the Triangle area. This isn't even a complete list."

"Do you think one of these has the box?" Rich cried.

"Wow—I had no idea," I told Jesse, not looking at Rich. "Could I maybe get a copy of this list?"

He glanced at it, then shrugged. "Sure, there's nothing private about it. I'll make you a photocopy."

When he left, I turned to Rich and grinned. "Maybe we can find out what Louise put in that box after all."

"Hello—can I help you please?"

I turned around. A man in glasses and a three-piece suit stood in the doorway. I looked up at him and realized he had an unfriendly expression on his face. "Uh, no, thank you, sir. Mr.—" For a moment I couldn't remember Jesse's last name. "—Temple is helping me."

The man glanced at the potato chips and caramels on the desk, and the suit jacket on the chair behind it, and his frown deepened. "Mr. Temple is only an assistant," he said.

"Well, he found me everything I needed to know," I said, picking up the piece of paper with the notes about the Chamblee family.

Before the man could say anything else, Jesse was back. "Here, I've got that list for you—" Then he saw the other man. "Oh, Mr. Morley, I didn't realize you were back." He practically shoved the papers into my hands, grabbing his jacket and trying to push the bags of chips and caramels back into the drawer at the same time.

"Thanks," I said, as half a dozen chips slid off the desk and onto the floor.

While the man glared through his glasses at the chips, Jesse glanced quickly at me and jerked his head toward the door.

Rich and I were halfway down the hall before Mr. Morley realized I was gone. I heard, "Who was that boy, Temple? And what did you think you were doing?"

"When you said I should stay in during lunch, sir, you also told me I needed to work more with the public," Jesse told him. "He's the public, isn't he? He had a school research project."

I couldn't just leave Jesse to get in trouble like that after he'd helped me so much, so I signaled to Rich to wait and hurried back to where Jesse was standing. "Thanks again, Mr. Temple," I said.

Jesse was trying to pick up potato chips under the man's disapproving look, so I added, "I'm sorry I made a mess with the potato chips." I turned to Mr. Morley, who was looking from Jesse to me now. "I'm sorry, sir, I guess I wasn't supposed to eat in the building. I won't do it again. But Mr. Temple really helped me a lot."

"Oh." The man looked surprised. "Well, see that you don't bring any food into the building again, young man. I'm glad to hear that Mr. Temple was able to help."

Jesse grinned at me and waved good-bye.

"What does the list say?" Rich demanded.

I glanced at the pages Jesse had given me. "Too much," I told him. "We're going to have to make some phone calls."

"Phone calls?" asked Rich.

I knew the calls to Raleigh would be long-distance from the Hambricks' house, and I didn't want Mrs. Hambrick to see anything on the phone bill, so I turned the money Dad had given me into a bunch of change and started making calls right there from a pay phone in the mall. Jesse's list had addresses and phone numbers, and I figured I could cross off a lot of possibilities with some fast phone calls.

"Finding these historical museums was a great idea, Red," Rich said, after I finally got him to understand that a telephone was a way of talking to a person miles away. "But why aren't we just going to see them?"

"Because there's like a hundred of them," I told him. "I can't look in every museum for your box. Besides, we only want places that got stuff from the construction sites at Research Triangle Park. They can tell me that over the phone."

I got depressed pretty soon at how right I was. Two hours, thirty-five phone calls, and nearly fifteen dollars later, I'd found only three of the little history museums in the Raleigh area that had gotten anything from the Park, and all they had were minié balls, a couple of broken bayonets, and some

Union uniform buttons. No small metal boxes, and nothing that would fit inside a box like that unless Louise had decided to save minié balls or Union buttons.

"What happened to it?" Rich asked, thumping the butt of his musket above the ground. He looked disheveled and frustrated, even though I was the one who'd been doing all the calling. Two ladies carrying shopping bags had glared at me when I'd banged down the phone receiver and immediately shoved in more money and punched in a new number. I just turned my back on them and kept calling—they could find another pay phone if they tried. I was frustrated at not learning anything.

Rich looked at me and pushed his hair back out of his face. Something about the gesture looked familiar, but I couldn't put my finger on it, and I glared at the phone. I punched in one more number, but the line didn't answer. That made six no-answers, three museums with buttons and bayonets but nothing worthwhile from Research Triangle Park, and twenty-seven people who told me they hadn't received anything from the Park construction at all. What a waste! Some of them hadn't even gotten anything in the last forty years— talk about historical.

"If we can't find it in one of the Durham museums," I told Rich, "you can come back and check out the ones that didn't answer. But we've got to get back to the bus stop. If I'm not home before supper, Dad's never going to let me out of his sight again."

I was almost right. We caught the 4:30 bus, but it was nearly 6:00 before we got all the way to the Hambricks' house. Supper wasn't ready yet, and Dr. Seagraves hadn't arrived, but Dad was already mad.

"Where have you been?" he demanded. "We've been back here for ages, and Nicole said you hadn't come home."

Nicole was standing behind him, looking smug. Maybe if I'd actually found something out with Richeson, I'd have felt better, but Dad's anger coming on top of my frustration made me angry right back. "You said I could do some sightseeing on my own, since you were too busy to take me yourself, remember?"

But he was too mad to be distracted by a guilt trip. "Don't you understand I was worried about you?" he snapped.

"Why?" I snapped right back. "You were fine with Mrs. Hambrick and Mr. Carey, weren't you? If you were so worried, why did you bring me here and just forget about me, anyway?"

"I never forgot about you—"

I didn't let him finish. "Look, I'm back before supper, okay? And it's still light out. So just let me wash up before Dr. Seagraves gets here."

Rich followed me upstairs slowly. "I don't understand, Alexander. Your father was upset because he was worried about you. But why are you so angry with him? Because he brought you to North Carolina? Because he didn't take you sightseeing?"

He sounded just like the school counselor, and I glared at him. "I'm angry with my dad because he's here with that woman—because he wants to marry her because he doesn't believe Mom's ever coming back! I'm angry with him because he wants to take me away from Indiana, so she'll never find me when she does come home. Okay? Give me a break—I've got a right to be angry!"

Rich was silent, but only for a moment. "But your father stayed with you. Not this afternoon, of course—but you knew you would see him this evening. Your mother is the one who left. If you're going to be angry with someone, why not her?"

"Are you angry at your mother for dying?" I demanded. "Are you angry at Louise for leaving? Is that why you want to find her, so you can haunt her great-grandkids or something and let everyone know how angry you are?"

Rich shook his head. "I'm not the one who's angry. I miss my mother, but she couldn't help dying. And I don't believe Louise wanted to go. That's why she left me a message." He looked down. "I only want to know that she was safe."

I threw the towel back on the rack and went down to be polite to Dr. Seagraves. Rich was wrong. I *wasn't* angry at Mom for leaving me. I'd told the counselor the same thing. And I had every right to be angry with Dad. What I hadn't told Rich was that I was angry with myself, too, for not helping him better. It didn't seem to matter how hard I tried—I couldn't get Dad to go home, I couldn't help Rich, and I couldn't be good enough for Mom.

———

Chapter Twelve

MAKING AN
INTERNET CONNECTION

"How come you go out and run so early every morning?" asked Carleton when I got back to the house the next morning. I climbed the stairs toward his bedroom, my legs heavy and aching.

"Because I'm on the track team," I told him.

"Then why don't you run with the rest of the team?" he asked.

"Because they're all back in Indiana," I said, pulling off my T-shirt and dropping it on the floor in his room.

"So, if you were home, you'd run with the team?" He picked up the shirt for me and tossed it in the hamper.

"In the afternoons we have track. In the mornings we all run on our own." I started doing my cooldowns.

"What are you doing now?"

I groaned. Couldn't he give it a rest with the questions? "I have to cool down after I run—slow my heartbeat and everything."

"Oh. If you got up a little later," Carleton said, "I could run with you."

"Um . . . you couldn't keep up—I run fast." I only sprinted on the last stretch, but I didn't tell him that.

"Do you always run alone?" he asked, looking disappointed. "It seems a funny kind of team if you do it all alone."

"I run with my dad sometimes," I said, but I was thinking Carleton was a sharp kid. I hadn't really thought about it like that, but that was why I'd gotten into track, instead of playing baseball or football—I didn't want to be part of a team that always does things together. I wanted to do something where I could be on my own and no one would bother me about being a loner.

"He hasn't been running with you here," Carleton said.

Thanks, kid, I thought. "Yeah, I noticed. He's been sleeping late—on vacation, I guess."

"Aren't you on vacation?"

I opened the door to the bathroom to take my shower. "If you're serious about running," I told him, "your legs can't ever take a vacation."

He laughed at that, and I found myself smiling as I stood under the hot water. It would have been neat to have a kid brother. I wondered why Mom and Dad hadn't had any other kids.

I let the shower wash that thought out of me. When I came back into the bedroom to get dressed, Carleton was gone, but Rich was sitting on my unmade bed.

"Hi," I said, pulling on my jeans and sitting on Carleton's neatly made bed to lace up my running shoes. "Look, about last night—"

"It's all right," he said.

"Thanks," I told him, and meant it. "Listen—it's too early to call the museums, but I had another idea. One of your brothers might have survived the War and had children later. And maybe one of them would know what happened to Louise."

Rich jumped up from my bed. "That's an excellent idea!" Then his face fell. "But how could we find their children—or great-great-grandchildren by now?"

I smiled at him. "Remember those computers I was telling you about yesterday? Well, they can do more than figure. They can send information back and forth to one another—instantly."

I didn't see Dad downstairs when we went into the room where he was staying. He was probably with Mrs. Hambrick somewhere, talking about how great the interview had gone. His laptop lay on the desk, and I turned it on. The window looking out on the oak trees was closed, but I could hear the wind chimes tinkling faintly beyond it. One was a collection of math symbols; the other was a group of different musical instruments. I remembered her saying that her husband had liked music—opera, wasn't it? I wondered if it was something they had enjoyed doing together. It was funny. I could think of all kinds of things Mom and I did together, but I couldn't think of much she did with Dad.

Rich watched the screen intently as it lit up, the light from the sleek PowerBook heightening the bones of his thin face. I could see the start-up icons reflected in his hopeful eyes.

"You know how the counties did a census?" I asked him, and he nodded. "Well, that created a list of information about people. There's all kinds of information stored in computers, and I can access the lists we want through this one."

I launched Dad's Internet browser. I went to the online white pages search engine and typed in "Chamblee," not specifying a state. In a few seconds, the screen told me I had 1,155 matches. "That's a lot of Chamblees."

"That's a wonder!" Rich said, smiling at the address listings on the screen.

I started printing out the list for Rich. Then I went back to the Search page and added "George" as a first name. "If your dad named George after himself, maybe your brother named his son George and they kept handing the name down."

Rich nodded intently. "I'm sure he would have."

But the screen showed me only five George Chamblees in the whole United States. Two were in Texas, and one was as far away as Alaska! The closest ones were in Alabama and Virginia.

"What about Jefferson?" Rich asked, as I clicked on Print. The search engine couldn't find any Jeffersons at all, but

I got ten Jeffs—a cluster of them in Mississippi, three in Alabama, one in Maryland, one all the way out in California—and one just over in Raleigh!

"That's it!" Rich cried.

"Maybe," I said, printing this list, too. "Let's call him."

I hoped Mrs. Hambrick wouldn't make a fuss over one long-distance call on her bill. And it was a little after nine, so I didn't think it was too early. I just hoped he wasn't at work.

It turned out I didn't have to worry. That Jeff Chamblee was a student at North Carolina State University, and his first class wasn't until eleven.

"Wow," he said, not too mad I woke him up. "Searching for some soldier's family from the Civil War? Hey—I'd like to help, but I can't. I'm from Kansas. I just came to school here because my girlfriend did. But good luck!"

At least he hadn't yelled at me.

I sighed, crossed his name off the list, and did a search for Chamblees with any first name who lived in North Carolina. There turned out to be 171 of them—plenty to keep Rich busy checking out for years to come. There were 27 in Raleigh, though I was afraid some of them were just going to be students, too.

"People move around a lot," I tried to explain to Rich. I thought of my dad interviewing at Research Triangle Park yesterday. "They don't just settle down in a house or on a farm or something and stay there forever. They live somewhere a few years, then change jobs and move. I've got kids in my class who've been to half a dozen schools!"

He shook his head. "It doesn't sound like a good way to live. How can you put down roots anywhere?"

I shrugged. I picked up Dad's Space Warrior and turned him over in my hand, rubbing the cool metal with one finger. "People don't think that's so important these days, I guess."

Rich sighed. "What about that one?" he asked, pointing to the screen.

One Chamblee actually lived in Durham. Nowhere near the original farm, of course, but it was possible a descendant had come home. I put down the Space Warrior and punched in the number.

This time a woman answered the phone, and I could hear kids shouting and crying in the background.

"Of course he's not here," she said sharply. "He's gone to work."

"I'm sorry, ma'am," I said. "It's for a research project for school. I'm supposed to find out about this family that lived here during the War Between the States named Chamblee? And I was hoping your husband might be descended from them."

"Around here?" She laughed, and it didn't sound like a nice laugh. "No, kid—we moved here from New Jersey because he got this great job in the Research Triangle. And days like today, I wish we'd never left."

I hung up and crossed that name off the list. Two names down and 1,153 to go.

"I can't call every person on this list," I told Rich. "I'm really sorry. I never thought we'd find so many Chamblees." I swallowed, wondering how many Thomsons there must be in Indiana, let alone the whole United States.

"I know—it was a good idea," Rich said, looking forlornly at the stack of paper from the printer. "I can travel to find them, starting with the others who live in North Carolina. When I see them, I'll know if they have the family features." He sighed. "But it won't help if Louise married and had children whose names we don't know."

I knew he was right.

Rich set aside his musket and reached into his knapsack. He took out something folded in a piece of oiled cloth. "What's that?"

"Just my journal," he said. "It's the only paper I have to write these down."

"You can take the list," I said, pushing it over to him, but he shook his head.

"Remember? I can't hold anything in your time. I'll have to copy them."

I watched him open his journal. It wasn't the sort of journal we keep at school, in bound books with mottled black-and-white covers, or even some kind of spiral notebook. It was really just a stack of paper with a couple of holes punched through one side and bolts driven down through the holes. Some sheets weren't even regular paper, but trimmed-down squares of wallpaper, or pages with printing on one side that might have been cut out of a book.

Rich saw me looking and smiled sadly. "I had plenty of paper for writing before the War. But paper got scarcer and scarcer. I used the better stuff to write home to Louise, but I kept this for the things I didn't write her. And since then— well, I've used it when I just needed to get something out."

He blushed a little and turned to a blank page near the end.

"It'll take you all day to write those names." And all the rest of your paper, I thought, but I didn't want to say that. I was sure he knew. And maybe he figured he wouldn't need any more paper if he found a family descendant.

He pulled out a worn stub of a pencil. "About as long as it takes you to call those museums," he answered, pointedly. "What I don't finish this morning I can finish tonight if you'll leave the pages spread out for me."

I nodded and set out several pages for him to work on. It was ten o'clock and the museums were opening, so I started on the local phone calls, moving the pages of the printout as Rich copied them.

He had almost finished the list for New York by the time I called all the Durham numbers Jesse had given me. Two of the museums had gone out of business, and most of the others had never gotten anything from anyone involved in Research Triangle Park. Some of them didn't have any War Between the States artifacts at all; they specialized in colonial things or vintage clothing. But most of them had stuff from the War, especially from Sherman's March, and they sounded proud of it. Two of the women I spoke with actually sounded insulted that their museum had been left out if there was anything worth getting from Research Triangle Park.

By the time I got to the end of the list, I'd only found seven museums that had received anything from the Park. Three of them had nothing but minié balls, broken bayonets, dented belt buckles, and uniform buttons, like the museums I'd talked to in Raleigh. Things like that were easy to find with metal detectors. But you'd think a metal detector would find the box Louise had left, too. The people I'd talked to at the other four museums told me they had gotten some very nice surprises from the construction people at the Park. They were probably exaggerating, but it gave us hope.

"Let's grab some lunch and hit the road," I told Rich, slipping the list and my pencil into a pocket, and running upstairs to stuff the printout in my duffel bag. Since Dad had given me money to pay for everything yesterday, I had enough of my own money to cover bus fare today. I hoped it wouldn't cost much to get into the museums.

It turned out everybody was grabbing lunch at the same time I got to the kitchen. Carleton was microwaving a hot dog, Nicole was eating some peaches and cottage cheese, and Dad and Mrs. Hambrick were making a chef's salad.

"Want some?" Dad offered.

Mrs. Hambrick added, "There's plenty—Nicole and Carleton decided they didn't want any."

Carleton beamed at me. "Want a hot dog?"

I shook my head. "Thanks, but I'll pass. Peanut butter and marmalade will do."

Nicole groaned and made a face around a mouthful of cottage cheese. And she thought peanut butter and marmalade looked disgusting!

Dad waited until I finished making my sandwich to say, "I'm afraid Paige and I have to go back to Triangle Park today. Mr. Carey asked for a follow-up meeting."

He was spending way too much time alone with Mrs. Hambrick, I thought. And I didn't like the fact that Mr. Carey wanted Dad to come back. But at least Rich and I could get out to the museums with no trouble.

Then Dad dropped the bombshell. "So Nicole's going to show you around instead."

—◦◦◦〜◦◦◦—

Chapter Thirteen

UNEXPECTED
COMPANY

I nearly dropped my sandwich. Nicole speared a chunk of peach and looked virtuous.

"Uh, that's okay," I stammered. "She doesn't have to. I mean—I did fine by myself yesterday."

"That's what we're worried about," Dad said, picking the ham out of his salad and eating it separately. "It kind of spooked me when you didn't turn up yesterday afternoon."

"I got back all right, didn't I?" I had to come up with a reason to be on my own today, or I'd never solve Rich's problem. And once I took care of Rich, I had my own problems to solve. I felt like I was juggling all these different hopes in the air and they were all going to come crashing down any minute.

"I know," Dad said, looking at me earnestly, "but I'd feel better if you had some company."

Well, I did have company, I thought. But I couldn't see Dad feeling any better if he knew I was wandering around with a ghost.

"I don't need any company," I said, but nobody paid attention.

"I'm coming, too!" Carleton piped, squirting mustard on his hot dog.

"It's going to be a family outing," Nicole said, smiling sweetly at her mother. I figured she was racking up points for something later on.

"Yes, it will," Mrs. Hambrick said. "And perhaps tomorrow the whole family can be together."

"Um." Nicole paused and studied her cottage cheese. "I thought we talked about my spending *some* time with the family and *some* time with my friends."

"They'd certainly be welcome to join us," Mrs. Hambrick said. As she turned away, Nicole made a face to her back, then shoved another peach in her mouth.

Rich stood as if leaning against the dining room wall, his musket propped against his chest, looking from one speaker to another.

"Why not just let them come with us, Alexander?" he suggested.

I couldn't answer in front of them. That was the big problem with having company while we hit the museums—I really needed to talk to Rich, and I couldn't do that unless I wanted Nicole to think I was crazy.

"Look, Dad," I started, but he didn't let me finish.

"Please, Alexander. I'll feel a lot better knowing you're not alone, okay? This way I'll be able to concentrate on the meeting." He looked at me, and I could see honest concern in his eyes. I sighed and picked up the last piece of my sandwich.

After Dad and Mrs. Hambrick left, I turned to Nicole. "I know this isn't your idea, and it isn't my idea, so let's just go our own ways. When they get back, we can tell them we hung out together—they won't know the difference."

She smirked. "Nice try, but you obviously have never had a kid brother." She nodded to Carleton, who was watching us. "He'll tell."

Carleton grinned up at me.

"Come on, Carleton," I said, "you wouldn't tell, would you?"

He nodded. "Unless you take me running with you tomorrow morning."

I sighed. But Carleton didn't give me a chance to make that choice. "I really want to go with you this afternoon," he said wistfully. Tomorrow probably sounded like a long time away to him.

"Even if you bribe him, he'll tell," Nicole said.

"Sounds like the voice of experience," I told her.

"So how about the mall?" she suggested.

"So how about some historical museums?" I countered.

"What?" she demanded, tugging on her hair. "You acted like you couldn't care less about history when Mom dragged us to Petersburg on Saturday. Now suddenly you're this big Civil War fan. I'm going to the mall."

"Okay," I said. "See you guys this evening."

"Mom's going to be mad if you go off alone," Nicole warned. "So's your dad."

"Maybe, but you were supposed to show me around. I don't think the mall is what your mom had in mind."

"I'm not into museums."

"This isn't the artsy kind where you have to look at paintings," I promised. "They're history museums. And they're little ones, so we'll be out fast."

"Will there be more cannons? And trenches?" asked Carleton.

Nicole got up, shoved the cottage cheese container in the refrigerator, and slammed the door.

"Trust me—they won't take long. Once we've seen them, we can go to the mall in whatever time's left over."

"What about the cannons?" Carleton repeated.

"Maybe," I told him. "We won't know until we go there and look inside."

"Okay," he said, smiling.

"I'm not wasting all afternoon in dusty little museums," Nicole said flatly.

"Just think how impressed your mother will be," I reminded her.

She considered that and said finally, "As long as we get to the mall."

"Deal."

When we were out of earshot of the kitchen, Rich asked, "What's wrong with having her come along, Red? She could be helpful."

"She could be, but she's not. Anyway—the problem is talking to you when they're around. To them it looks like I'm talking to myself."

Rich frowned. "I wish I could make other out-of-timers see me or hear me."

"I can imagine Nicole's face if she saw a ghost!" I said. But the sudden surge of jealousy surprised me. I didn't want Nicole or Carleton to see Rich—he was *my* friend!

As we waited at the bus stop, Nicole said, "I'm surprised you're not tagging along with your dad, trying to do something to break things up with my mother."

I shrugged. "I don't see what I could do." Except get him back home and refuse to move here, I thought. No point in telling her that, though.

"You don't say much, but I've seen the way you look at my mom. I mean—it's so obvious you can't wait to drag your dad out of her clutches."

I couldn't help laughing, and Nicole grinned. "Well—I mean, what gives? Your mom walked out on you, right? Why can't your dad look at someone else?"

I stopped laughing. "My mom's coming back."

She was silent for a minute. Then she said, "Sometimes you sound just like Carleton. It doesn't matter what you tell him, he's got his own idea of the truth."

"The bus is coming!" shouted Carleton, racing down the sidewalk.

I watched the bus shudder to a stop directly in front of us. "Looks like Carleton's got a pretty good grasp of the truth to me," I told her.

Then I climbed on and found a seat. I even remembered to sit in the back so that she wouldn't question my story about getting carsick. That worked out great, because she sat up near the front and Rich and I sat together.

The museums were all downtown. The first one wasn't too exciting—it was dark, with cobwebs in the corners. Nicole rolled her eyes the minute we opened the door. Even Carleton looked disappointed. And all they had from Research Triangle Park were some regimental buttons and a battered canteen. I hoped the other museums would be better, or Nicole was going to drag me off to the mall before we saw them all.

The second museum was in an old brick house that had been restored. I could see a blue painted rocking chair with flowered cushions on the wooden porch. Beyond it, a screen door led into the hallway where a woman sat behind a little desk, reading a book. She looked up and smiled as we stepped onto the porch.

"Can I help you?" She wore a denim skirt and sneakers, and a bright gold T-shirt that said "Keep the Past Alive! Support Durham County History" with a name tag pinned to it that read "Sarah Edwards."

I smiled at her. "Hi, Ms. Edwards—I'd like to keep the past alive."

She laughed. "Well, if you like the shirt, you can buy one! We don't charge admission, so that's one of the ways we stay in business—selling T-shirts and history books and key-chains—all those sorts of goodies."

I grinned and explained what I was doing there. "I was over at Research Triangle Park the other day and saw all the construction going on—and I figured they must have turned up lots of stuff that had been around since the War Between the States."

"They certainly did!" Ms. Edwards agreed. "Our founder has friends who worked for one of the construction crews, and they brought us a lot of terrific things. We haven't sorted it all out yet. The artifacts that are on display are over in that area." She looked from me to Nicole. "Is this pure love of history, or a project for school?"

Nicole shrugged. "Ask him, not me. It's *his* project." She wandered over to look at a colonial house exhibit, showing mannequins dressed up and arranged as if they were sitting down to a meal.

"Your sister looks more interested in colonial history than the War."

"She's more interested in going to the mall," Carleton told Ms. Edwards before I could set her straight about Nicole not being my sister. "But I'm interested in history. Do you have any cannon here?"

"Oh, I'm afraid not," Ms. Edwards said. "But we do have some muskets and bayonets. Would you like to see those?" He followed her happily.

More bayonets, I thought, heading over to the area where the stuff from the Park was supposed to be. At least this place was better than the first museum we tried.

"Alexander—come quickly! You have to get it out for me! It's here!"

Rich's hand grabbed for me desperately, and his touch seared my elbow. My whole arm went numb and got thick and heavy. I stifled a cry and Rich let go, shocked, as if he hadn't been aware of what he'd done. Hot pinpricks of feeling danced up and down my arm.

"I'm sorry! I didn't mean to hurt you—but it's here!"

The others were busy, so I said in a low voice, "All right already—where is it?"

"Over here!" He pointed to a display cabinet in a corner, and I followed him, rubbing my tingling arm.

"I don't see any box—"

And then I saw it, even before Rich's jabbing finger slid through the glass as if it were a wall of water and tapped at the object inside the case. It was a silver locket, open, hanging from a pin stuck through a loop that would have held a necklace chain. Even if Rich hadn't said anything, I'd have known this was what we were looking for. The woman in the locket's miniature portrait had thick black hair, like Rich's, and expressive black eyes that seemed to burn across the years. Beneath it, a card read: "Locket belonging to the Chamblee family, circa 1860."

"So that's what Louise left for you," I said softly. "Not a note where she was going, but her locket."

"My mother's locket," Rich said quickly. "Louise treasured it and would only wear it on special occasions. I don't understand how she could leave it behind."

"I guess she wanted you to have it," I said. I studied the portrait. There was something familiar about the face—probably the resemblance to Rich.

Coiled in the other side of the open locket was a black lock of hair. Was it Louise's hair, or their mother's? Then I read the card beside the locket again. "Wait a minute—was Louise's name or your mother's name on the locket?"

"No," Rich said, shaking his head. "Neither one."

"Then Louise must have left you something else inside the box—something signed." I pointed to the card. "How else would they have known the name?"

"She must have written a note and signed it! But where could it be?" Rich cried, looking around frantically. His hair fell into his eyes and he brushed it back.

"I see you found the Research Triangle Park's greatest treasure, at least from our point of view," said Ms. Edwards.

"Ask her!" demanded Rich. "She must know where the note is!"

"It's beautiful," I said, honestly. "She still looks—so alive."

"It's a miracle," Ms. Edwards said simply. "Especially considering the condition we found it in!"

"Where's the note?" Rich cried. He was looking through all the cases.

"What do you mean?" I asked, hoping he'd figure out I was getting to that, but I couldn't ask her directly without making her wonder how I knew about the box in the tree in the first place.

"This wasn't something the construction crew dug up," she explained. "It was tucked away in a hole in an old oak tree, of all places! They found it when they were cutting the tree up as they cleared the land."

"Really?" I tried to sound surprised. "How did you know who the locket belonged to? Did it have a name on it?"

"Not on the locket itself, but the locket wasn't alone." She smiled. "It wouldn't have survived all that time on its own. No—whoever put it there wrapped it in a piece of heavy paper first. We think it must have been a strip of wallpaper."

Rich's head whipped around.

"They also used the clean side of the wallpaper to write something," she went on. "My guess is that it was left for a soldier coming back from the War, who wouldn't know what had happened to the family—perhaps a relative, or a sweetheart."

"What did the note say?" I could scarcely keep the excitement out of my voice.

Ms. Edwards looked puzzled. "Why are you so interested in this discovery?"

"Well," I began, wondering what to say.

"He loves history," Carleton said. "He got excited when we went to Petersburg. They shot off a real cannon—Pow! Alexander almost got sick, he was so excited!"

Thanks, I thought. Now she'd never tell me anything.

"What have you found this time?" Nicole asked. "Hey—this locket's cool."

Ms. Edwards smiled, and she looked relaxed again. "It sounds as though you're quite the history buff—Alexander, was it?"

"Yes, ma'am," I admitted.

"Well, Alexander, I'm afraid the note was barely legible. It was wrapped around the locket, then the two of them were placed in a tin box. The box was sealed quite tightly and would have kept them safe for several years, but over time the tin deteriorated and water seeped in." Ms. Edwards sighed. "By the late 1860s it was hard to get ink in the South, and many people made their own from a mixture of lamp-black—that's the soot left over from a kerosene lantern—and linseed oil. That ink smeared when the paper got wet, so parts of it were badly smudged."

"Could I see the note?" I asked, mentally crossing my fingers.

"Oh, it's not out on display," she said. "It was too badly damaged."

"But you must have cleaned it up enough to read at least part of it," I said. "You didn't just throw it away after that, did you?"

Rich gasped at the thought.

"Of course not!" Ms. Edwards looked shocked, too. "It's stored between plates of glass in the back. But that room isn't open to the public."

I looked at the locket again and at the reflection of Rich's desperate face in the display case. I turned back to Ms. Edwards. "I can't explain it," I said, which was true enough. "But there's something about that woman's picture." And about the ghost who looked so like her, I thought to myself. "I'd *really* like to see that note."

Ms. Edwards hesitated a moment longer. Then she said, "Well, why do we have these things if people can't see them? That's what I hate about big museums—they always keep the best treasures locked away." She looked around as if someone were about to sneak up on us. Then she grinned. "Can you two keep a lookout?"

Nicole just studied the portrait, playing with her hair thoughtfully.

"Sure!" Carleton shouted.

Ms. Edwards led me through a door behind a display of Confederate uniforms and flags, and Rich followed, his pale face full of hope and drawn with fear. She switched on a bright overhead light and pulled open a shallow metal drawer in a wide cabinet. There were other things in the drawer, but she carefully lifted out two pieces of glass, with Louise's note sandwiched in between them.

I heard a hiss of indrawn breath from Rich and felt a cool breeze shudder through the room. Ms. Edwards looked around nervously and tried to smile, but I could see she was afraid that something was wrong. I bent over the glass plates quickly.

I could barely make out the writing on the torn piece of wallpaper. As Ms. Edwards said, the ink had faded and was blurred where it had been partially washed away. The top line looked something like: *My d r   bro er.*

After that I could only make out single words, or parts of words:

h rm	*gone*	*drew*	*etter*
Bake	*Ill no*	*airo*	*sur*
ait fo	*appro*	*eet*	*oth loc*
our ey			

I couldn't even guess at anything else until the bottom of the paper—the right side was the clearest. I guessed that corner must have been wrapped closest to the locket.

L v   Lou se Chamblee

Tw   St r   M rc   29th 186

Beside me, Rich whispered, "I can't make out anything but her name and the date." His voice broke. "Except, perhaps, 'My dear brother.'"

Chapter Fourteen

RICH'S JOURNAL

"I was too late," said Rich numbly, following me out of the back room. "If I'd been able to open the box sooner, I could have read the message. Now I'll never know what happened to her. Suppose she hid the note and the Yankees—" he swallowed, "killed her?"

"So what did you find out?" Nicole asked me. She actually sounded faintly interested.

I shook my head. "Only what it says in the display—the name and the date."

Ms. Edwards sighed. "It's so frustrating to know that history was right there waiting for you, and if someone had only found it earlier we'd know its secrets."

Beside her Rich clenched one fist helplessly, and she shivered. "Is it cold in here?"

Nicole glanced at me, eyebrows raised.

"A little, I guess," I said. "Thanks for letting me see the note, Ms. Edwards."

She smiled. "You're quite welcome, Alexander. It's wonderful to see kids like you caring so much about history."

"I care!" Carleton told her.

"Of course. You all make quite a team of historians," she told him.

Nicole started for the door.

I took one last look at the portrait of Rich's mother in the locket. "Locket belonging to the Chamblee family, circa 1860." I wondered why it didn't read 1865, and remembered that the year had been unclear in the date on Louise's note. Only the "186" came through, so they must have known it was left there sometime in that decade.

"Thanks again," I told Ms. Edwards, and I bought a "Keep the Past Alive! Support Durham County History" T-shirt on our way out.

"You want to let me in on this thing you do with the cold?" Nicole asked as we waited for the bus to the mall.

I tugged at the ends of the braided lariat on my wrist. "I don't do anything."

"Oh yeah? Well, that woman in the museum felt it today, and I sure felt it the other night. Carleton did, too, and I think even Mom and your dad noticed."

Carleton looked up. "And the chimes keep ringing all of a sudden," he said.

Nicole nodded. "Nothing like that ever happened before you showed up. So what gives?"

"Nothing like that ever happened back home in Indiana either," I told her, which was true. "I think you've got a weird climate or something."

Fortunately, the bus came just then, and I went straight to the back, leaving Nicole and Carleton near the front.

Rich sat beside me, shaking his head. "It was all for nothing," he said bitterly. "All that fighting—we didn't win, and I didn't keep Louise safe. I should never have left Two Stirrups."

He looked so miserable sitting there that I wished I could punch him on the arm like I'd do if a runner on the team lost a race he'd expected to win. But I couldn't. "I'm sorry," I whispered instead, not caring if anybody on the bus thought I was talking to myself. But I could feel just how useless those words were.

I trailed after Nicole at the mall. Rich had said he'd wait at the bus stop, and I hoped he was okay. I wished I could have just sat there with him, instead of feeling lost in this maze of stores.

"I liked that museum," Carleton said unexpectedly, as if he knew I felt down.

I managed a smile. "I did, too," I told him.

"It had neat things, even if it didn't have a cannon."

I nodded, and for once he seemed satisfied to walk along beside me, not asking questions.

Mrs. Hambrick couldn't believe Carleton and Nicole had gone to a museum.

"Two history places!" Carleton told her proudly.

"It was okay," Nicole said, shrugging, and her mother looked stunned. "So—I can spend tomorrow with my friends?" She flashed me a grin when she got an okay.

I didn't ask Dad how the meeting had gone, and he didn't volunteer any information. I was afraid that meant they'd offered him a job. I didn't want to hear that he'd accepted it.

Rich sat out on the porch during supper. I heard him play his harmonica softly for a little while—a sad tune I didn't know. Then it got quiet. As soon as I helped clear the table, I went upstairs to get my recorder.

"Alexander," Dad said as I came downstairs with it.

"I'm kind of tired, Dad," I told him, before he got started. "I thought I'd just play my recorder a while and turn in."

He looked disappointed, but nodded. Maybe he didn't really want to tell me about the job any more than I wanted to hear about it.

When I got out to the porch, Rich was sitting cross-legged with his journal open on his lap and his musket lying by his side.

"What were you playing?" I asked.

He smiled faintly in the twilight. "An old song, called 'The Volunteer.'"

"I didn't recognize the melody."

He picked up his harmonica and played it again. I put my recorder together and tried to follow along.

At the end, I asked, "What are the words?"

158

His voice was a strong, clear baritone that rang out in the quiet evening:

I leave my home and thee dear,
With sorrow in my heart.
It is my country's call, dear,
To aid her I depart.

And on the blood-red battle plain
We'll conquer or we'll die.
'Tis for our honor and our name,
We raise the battle cry.

Then weep not, dearest, weep not,
If in her cause I fall.
O, weep not sister, weep not,
It is my country's call.

The last note hung in the air. Then he picked up his harmonica, and I took my recorder, and we played it through together. I didn't think I'd forget this one, even without writing down the notes.

Rich said bitterly, "Much good it did, dying on the battlefield. What honor was there in leaving my sister to face Sherman's men alone? My home gone, my name gone, around here anyway—except for eleven hundred strangers scattered all the way to California."

159

"That's not true," I told him. "You said you had to enlist—for your country and for your family."

He shook his head and picked up his journal. "I need to copy those names."

I looked at the sheets of paper bound by those bolts. He'd carried it all these years—into battle and beyond.

"What kind of stuff did you write in your journal?" I asked.

Rich shrugged a little. "Just—I don't know. I'd see things and think about them and write down what I thought. Some poetry—not very good, I'm afraid—letters home I didn't send."

"Why not?" I asked, surprised.

"Well . . . I wrote Louise all the time. But I didn't want to worry her. I'd joke with her about the friends I was making, and promise I was keeping the Yankees from reaching Richmond—single-handed!" His eyes lightened briefly. "I didn't tell her about the food and the rain and how many Yankees there were on the other side of the line. I had to tell someone, though, so I wrote in my journal like I was writing to her. I figured when I got home, I could tell her the truth and we could laugh about it then, when we were safe around the fire, with a good meal in our stomachs." He looked down and took a deep breath. "I'm sorry to have dragged you with me on this wild-goose chase, Alexander."

"We found the locket," I pointed out.

"But Louise's message is lost." He looked down at his

journal bleakly. "If she somehow survived, she must have despaired of me."

"She couldn't have!" My vehemence surprised me. "She must have realized what happened."

"I thank you for that kindness. Now—if you could lay out the pages with the names of my perhaps-relations, I'll get back to copying."

I found it hard to sleep, thinking of Rich outside bent over his journal, copying strangers' names in the hopes that one of them might know something about his sister from so long ago. Talk about a wild-goose chase! But the locket had told us so little. I lay there listening to Carleton's even breathing and reread the note in my mind. There was something about those word fragments.

I gave up on sleeping and got out of bed, pulled on my running clothes, and tiptoed downstairs. Rich was dozing on the porch. His journal floated just above the wood planks, where he had left it. I didn't want to wake him, so I reached down, not knowing what would happen. Would I be able to pick the journal up?

The pages felt cool and rough, like rippled slivers of ice. I couldn't hold the bound pages, but I found I could nudge the cold paper a little so the sheets fluttered, as if blown by a breeze. I sat down on the cool plank floor and read the spidery words that he hadn't gotten home to deliver.

Tired the men in grey.
Tired the men in blue.
Tired the folk at home,
Families split in two.

Glove of grey,
Glove of blue,
Are reaching out to shake.
Men in grey,
Men in blue,
Two neighbor lands to make.

It felt kind of strange to think of someone believing we'd be better off as two countries. We were one nation—families and nations should stay together, shouldn't they?

I nudged another page and felt the heat drain out of my fingers. I blew on my hand, then tucked it under my arm and read the letters Rich had never sent.

January 13
Dear Sister,
I have just mailed you a letter joking about playing in the mud puddles, the way we used to play when we were very small. I wish it were the same today. We stand in place behind the earthworks, our boots coming apart at the seams and the soles thin to the point of holes. We drill in the mornings, splashing through puddles, until our feet

are cold as chunks of ice in the creek. My boots have frozen stiff so many times they have rubbed my heels until my socks tear and every step burns. I thought we'd be issued new boots with the rest of our equipment, but there was hardly any equipment to issue, except for a musket and a cartridge box. Across the lines, we can hear the Yankees talking about their new uniforms. I shiver in my old coat and wish I'd taken my warmest good coat, but I thought I'd be back after Johnston stopped Sherman. I never imagined my old coat wearing so thin so fast.

January 30
Dear Sister,

How empty the house must be with only you and Amalie knocking around like a couple of lonely marbles in a schoolboy's jacket pocket. I sent you a letter telling you how proud I am that Father has been called out with the Home Guard, but the truth is that I wish he had stayed in the house to keep you and Amalie safe. I know General Johnston will stop Sherman's raiders, but I fear Yankee deserters fleeing through the countryside. Well, you will never read this unless I make it home safely, so I will admit to you that I also fear sometimes that Sherman and Grant are unstoppable. They have too many men in the Union Army. We stand here, ready to do our duty, and no one gives the order to attack. I fear they doubt we could even beat the Yankees.

February 19

My dear Sister,

 I would be very lonely here if it were not for Noah Langston. I have written you about him. He can never be so close a friend as you, but he is a good companion. I hope that you and Amalie have grown closer now that it is just the two of you at the farm. I will not mail this to you, because I can see Amalie turning up her nose at my advice on any subject! But I do not like to think of you alone. Perhaps she will tell you her secrets, now that it is just the two of you, and you can whisper them to me when I come home, and you and I will tease her, and she will roll her eyes and tell us what a pair of confounded nuisances we are.

March 3

Dearest Sister,

 I am writing by firelight as Noah and the others speak of their memories of home. I have always looked ahead to the future but now, like them, I find myself thinking more of the past. Do you remember Christmases when we were small and Mother was still alive? I stare into the fire's embers and see the tree on Christmas morning, decorated with paper cornucopias filled with candies and draped with ribbons and cranberry chains, with bulging stockings at the fireplace. There were no full stockings last Christmas, but we were together. I hear a soft harmonica melody drift past from another campfire and recall those nights in the parlor, before the War. I can hear Amalie playing the piano and Father singing. Poor George was always so frustrated that he could not sing a note—do you remember? But I can still hear his clear voice reciting poetry. I will not send this letter, for the memories do not comfort me as they should, and I think they would not comfort you, either.

March 12
Dearest Sister,

I lie at night wrapped in my thin bedroll that does so little to keep out the cold, and I close my eyes and see us all together again around the table at supper: Father carving, Amalie serving, you kicking your chair legs until Father or Amalie tells you to stop, George discussing politics with Father, and Jefferson and I arguing about plowing our land around the hills rather than up them. I remember special evenings when you and Jefferson and I would entertain the family. Can you remember those skits and pantomimes we worked so hard to make up? Sometimes I see Mother smiling and clapping for us, and then I know I've fallen asleep and am dreaming. But the rest of the time it's a wish, the only wish I have as we get closer and closer to a day when we must fight or retreat— the wish to see you again and for all of us to be together at Two Stirrups.

That entry was dated less than two weeks before Rich had lost his life at Fort Stedman. I looked at his sleeping face. All he'd wanted was to find out what had happened to his family, to Louise. And all I wanted was to find out where my mother was and what had happened to her.

There wasn't any way that I could undo the fact he'd died in the battle, of course. So there was no way he'd ever make that dream of sitting down at the dinner table with his family come true. But I'd been thinking about the locket and the note and the reasons that had drawn Rich and me together, and I had an idea. I wasn't sure if it would work, but I'd come up with a way that we might—just possibly—be able to find out what happened to Louise.

Chapter Fifteen

FACING THE YANKEES

It was still early when I got back from running, but Nicole was already in the kitchen toasting a bagel. That seemed to be her regular breakfast.

"You stink," she said.

"Good morning to you, too." I was nervous, but I'd made up my mind. I was going through with it. At least, I'd try. "Your mom was so impressed with your interest in history yesterday she said you could spend today with your friends, right?"

"No," she said flatly.

"No what? Did she say you couldn't after all?" I was going to carry out my plan no matter what, but if I could use Nicole to cover for me, Dad wouldn't be so worried.

"No, you can't come with us."

"Oh! I don't want to," I said with relief. "But I'm going to leave my dad a note saying I'm with you, okay? If he asks, could you just say I tagged along?"

She raised an eyebrow. "What are you up to anyway? More history museums?"

"Basically, yes," I told her, which wasn't really untrue—it was just stretching things a little.

"So tell me about this thing with the cold and maybe I will."

"I told you—it's not me."

Nicole bit into her bagel and crunched for a while. "Are you sure everything's okay, Alexander? You seem—kind of jumpy."

I looked up, surprised. What did she care? Anyway, she'd never believe me if I told her about Rich. "Everything's okay," I lied.

She stared at me for a minute, then shrugged. "Well, we're going to the movies, so we'll be back late. You'll have to make up a story about leaving us and coming home on your own."

"Thanks. I'll think of something," I told her, heading upstairs to shower. I dressed as quietly as possible and managed to sneak out of the room without waking Carleton.

I didn't see Nicole, so I quickly made myself a couple of sandwiches and wrapped them up to take with me. Then I grabbed a pencil and the magnetic pad stuck to the refrigerator and left a note:

Dad—

I had a good time with Nicole yesterday (surprise, surprise!). Thought I'd spend today the same way.

Guess you had a good time with Mrs. Hambrick, too,
so I hope you won't mind.

See you later, A.

It covered me so that Dad shouldn't worry too much, and it wasn't exactly a lie. I *was* going to spend today the same way I spent yesterday—helping a ghost.

Rich looked surprised when I woke him up on the porch.

"I have an idea," I said softly. "Come on."

He stuffed his journal into his knapsack and grabbed his musket. "What is it?"

I started around the house, nearly expecting Dad and Mrs. Hambrick to catch me. But we made it up the driveway, and I headed for the Duke bus stop with relief.

"What's this idea?" Rich asked again.

"Well, I couldn't sleep last night, and I was thinking about seeing you at Fort Stedman. You said you'd been waiting for me."

He nodded. "For an out-of-timer who could see me."

"Well," I asked, "was everybody in the battle waiting for me?"

He looked at me, surprised.

"In fact, did everyone I see there die that day?" I asked, remembering the Confederate troops who made it back across the cornfield and the Yankees who attacked the fort at the end. "I don't think so. I'm guessing I saw that battle because a bunch of things came together at the right time."

Now that I was talking about my plan, I felt calmer. "First of all, you needed someone to help you, and you said I was the right out-of-timer for you. Second, that was an important battle to the men who fought in it, so it was sort of stamped into their memories—the ones who lived, anyway. And the ones who died—well, you said yourself that there were others like you who came back to Fort Stedman because they had no place to rest. There were a lot of—I don't know—strong emotions, I guess, tied up with that event and with the place where it happened. So it kind of replays itself, over and over, until something stops the cycle."

Rich was nodding. "That all makes sense, but what good does it do us?"

"And third," I finished, "I didn't see you just any day—Saturday was the anniversary of the battle, and you told me you all 'experience' the battle again on each anniversary."

"It was—but I still don't see what you're getting at." He sounded frustrated.

"Remember Louise's note?" I asked him. "I know it wasn't very clear, but her name was and so was the date—most of it, anyway."

His eyes narrowed as he struggled to picture the note in his mind. Then they opened wide.

"March twenty-ninth is what her note said," I told him. "Today."

I saw the bus coming toward the stop and got out my fare. "We're going back to Research Triangle Park. It must have been an important day to Louise and Amalie, and to you, too, even though you weren't there. I'm betting that Louise needs someone to help her find out what happened to you as much as you need help finding out what happened to her— maybe I'm the right out-of-timer for her, too. And today's the twenty-ninth, so if it's going to work, it's got to be today."

The bus screeched to a halt and the doors wheezed open. I jumped on. Behind me, Rich climbed the steps more slowly. "Do you really think it can work?" he asked, his voice sounding as if he scarcely dared to hope.

I couldn't say anything but I nodded, and he broke into a broad smile.

The bus was packed with commuters, so Rich and I had to stand. Even in the crowd, other riders gave us a wide berth, and I wished I'd brought my sweatshirt. Rich was so excited, the cold was coming off him in waves, like the first time I met him.

We caught the morning shuttle from the Research Triangle Park bus center and got off one stop past the computer buildings.

"Shouldn't we go to the same place as the farm?" Rich asked, puzzled.

"As close as we can get," I told him. "But remember those guards? I don't think they'll want us hanging around waiting for history to repeat itself."

We crossed the street and walked back toward the construction site opposite the recreation area. There were plenty of trees there to keep us out of sight. It should be good enough if we were close to where Rich's tree had been. At least, I hoped so.

I sat down and unwrapped a sandwich while Rich paced. "Before I got to Fort Stedman," I said, "I heard a lot about the battle and the siege, at that museum and from Mrs. Hambrick. Maybe that helped me slip into your time." After all, the times I'd seen ghosts without knowing anything about their history, I hadn't stepped through the window. "So—tell me more about what it was like living at Two Stirrups."

He glanced down at me. "You mean during the War?"

I nodded.

Rich looked across the road at the recreation area thoughtfully. "The Yankees always talk about the South as if it was all one big, wealthy plantation. Two Stirrups was just a small farm. Things were better before the War, but I wouldn't say they were ever luxurious. After the Yankees blockaded our ports, we couldn't ship our crops abroad, so we didn't earn any money to buy food or anything."

I swallowed a bite of sandwich. "How did you get by?"

"We had to work harder to feed ourselves. We got a little butter and milk from the last of the cattle, though we shared that with the Bakers on the next farm over. And we had to grow vegetables in Amalie's flower beds. We made do with two meals most days—I could see Louise getting thinner, and that worried me."

Rich had gotten pretty thin himself, but I didn't say anything. The morning turned into afternoon as he told me how conditions worsened as the War dragged on. I watched guards drive through the building parking lots and shipping bays as trucks came to load circuit boards and whatever else they made there.

I wondered what time of day it was when Sherman's men came through the Chamblees' fields, burning their crops. Would we have to be there at the exact moment? I'd found Rich at Fort Stedman hours later than the dawn attack. Perhaps it could happen anytime. Perhaps it could happen now. But I didn't feel drawn anywhere as I'd been drawn to the Salient and then to Fort Stedman that day. And there were none of the signals that meant a ghost was nearby—except Rich, of course. Maybe my plan was no good.

Traffic picked up as people went home from work, and then quieted down as the offices closed, and the guards across the street made fewer passes in their trucks.

As twilight deepened, Rich said, "After the blockade tightened, we'd go to bed at darkfall, because we only had tallow candles to burn." He wrinkled his nose. "They were made from beef fat, and they stank like a frypan full of greasy bacon that had gone bad." He looked off into the distance. "Sometimes Louise and I would sit out on the porch in the moonlight. I'd play my harmonica and she'd sing. Or we'd just talk about our dreams for After the War—everything was After the War, because we were so miserable in the present. I thought that fighting would be better. At least I'd be doing something. But in the end it didn't matter."

"Yes, it did!" I said fiercely, surprising myself. I'd eased into the past along with Rich and now I cared about protecting his world and his family.

"It didn't matter to Louise," he said tiredly. "I wasn't there when she needed me."

"But she left you that note. I think she was proud of you for doing something." I stood up. Traffic had all but disappeared, and I could feel a strange pull urging my feet toward the buildings beyond the weeping willow trees. It was time to go.

I asked, "You said the house was past the willow trees and the lake, right? I'm going to see if anything happens as I get closer to the place."

As we crossed the road, I felt goosebumps rise along my arms. Had I thought it was cold around Rich these past few days? I began to feel I was in a January ice storm back home, and fumbled to button up my flannel shirt. Suddenly I nearly choked on the familiar orange smell.

I circled around the hedges, using the trees to shield me from sight. Rich walked through the branches, looking back and forth uncertainly.

"What's going on?" he asked. "I smell—oranges."

I opened my mouth to say, "Welcome to the world of

ghosts," even though I knew my voice would be shaky, but before I got the first word out I heard a shout.

"You, kid! What are you doing here? This is private property—no trespassing!"

Through the trees, I could see two guards running across the volleyball courts beyond the lake.

"Alexander!" Rich shouted.

I turned to run back across the street to the construction site, but my ankle caught in the tangled roots. I lost my balance and stumbled, falling toward the hedges, hearing more shouts behind me. I picked myself up and glanced back to see how close the guards were and ducked as I heard that strange popping whoosh of a gunshot, then another. Could they actually be shooting at me?

Smoke swept over me in gusts. The building behind the men with guns glowed red and yellow against the darkening sky—and the men in front of it weren't guards, but soldiers. Only a few of them were wearing proper uniforms, but there were enough dark blue jackets to mark them for Northern soldiers—Sherman's raiders! It wasn't the one-story computer building I had seen a minute ago. It was a two-story house. The white paint was already soot-stained by the fire, but I could make out the green door, hanging half open, and the green shutters I remembered from my dream. Beyond it, flames leaped through the wooden slats of a barn roof.

A young woman ran past me, clutching a pink and white quilt. She ran maybe six steps farther, and then a soldier carrying a swaying torch reached out and grabbed the trailing edge of the quilt. "Leave it!" the man snarled. "That's too good for a secesh the likes of you—freeze with the rest of you rebel scum!" He twisted the torch into the center of the quilt and threw the flaming mess on the ground.

"Private!" An officer wearing a blue uniform rode up to the soldier. "Leave the women alone!" He turned to Amalie. "Are you hurt, ma'am?"

"Amalie!" Rich cried as he ran to her, but she just hugged her dress around her and backed away from the two soldiers as if she didn't see her brother. Rich drew his bayonet from his scabbard and turned on the drunken soldier, twisting the blade into place on his musket. But the long three-edged bayonet passed through the soldier the way Rich had walked through the tree branches. This was 1865, but it wasn't his time—he'd been dead before Sherman's raiders reached his farm. More gunfire rang out behind the house, along with whoops and shouts.

"Teach these secesh a lesson," the soldier said, and ran to join the others.

The officer reached toward Amalie. Maybe he was trying to help her, but she turned from him and ran into the shadows. Rich followed a few steps, then stopped.

"The Bakers' farm is that way," he panted. "Maybe she's running to them for help—but the raiders must be headed there as well. I don't know if she'll be safe!"

"Where's Louise?" I demanded through chattering teeth.

In the night, the shouts of the men and the crackling of the fire were deafening. Something crashed in the barn and the roof caved in, and I wanted to shake Rich. There couldn't be much time left. "Have you seen her?"

He looked around wildly.

The tree, I thought. Louise would have gone to the oak tree in order to leave the locket for Rich. I turned back toward the cluster of trees at the construction site. In the fire's glow, I could see a much larger grove of trees there now, and I headed for it. In a moment, Rich joined me.

Then I saw Louise—a girl maybe a year older than me, wearing a dark calico dress, running back through the trees toward the house. A hair ribbon held back most of her black curls, but the right side had pulled loose and hung in her face. If she was coming back, she must have already hidden the locket.

Then out of the corner of my eye I noticed a soldier, mounted bareback on a horse. He had caught sight of her, too, and he kicked the horse, jerking its head around by pulling its mane. The horse stumbled, righted itself, and broke into a canter straight for Louise.

"No!" Rich screamed, running toward them, the flames glinting off his bayonet. I knew he'd never make it, and I remembered the way his blade just passed through the other soldier. Even if Rich reached the man, he wouldn't be able to stop him.

Rich knew it, too. "No!" he howled again, but it was a cry of desperation, with no strength in it.

I sprinted. Aiming just short of Louise, I hoped to catch the horse before the man was close enough to grab for her if I won this race. No warm-ups, no chance to get psyched—I just took every second of running I'd ever done, and every piece of coaching I'd ever gotten, and made it work for me. I kept my back straight, to open up my lungs, and used my arms to pump. I ran full-out, knees high, faster than I'd ever run on the school track.

I didn't even know if the man would see me, or feel me—but I had to try. And I remembered Fort Stedman. Rich had seen me, all right. I think a couple of the other men had as well. And I'd sure felt those cold hands prod me. I'd *been* there. I'd stepped into the past and become a part of the ghosts' time. I could do it again.

Barely ten yards before the soldier would have reached Louise, I crashed into the horse and grabbed on to its mane. My whole body felt chilled.

The man pulled up a fist to hit me, and I got a strong whiff of whiskey cutting right through the oranges. But trying to hit me meant he could see me! Maybe with my blue jeans and blue plaid shirt, I might fit in with the other soldiers in their ragged uniforms.

"Sir," I cried, dodging his fist and struggling to catch my breath. "Please, sir—the officer wants you."

The soldier squinted at me. "Who're you, boy? You look odd—what's that you're wearing?"

He hadn't bought it. Desperately, I groped for an explanation. "Um—my uniform—it was falling apart, sir. I grabbed some clothes from the house."

He still didn't look convinced. I suddenly remembered the drummer boy at Fort Stedman. He'd been sent with a message. Maybe that would distract the soldier from my appearance. "I'm the drummer boy, sir—my drum's over by the supplies. The officer ordered me to find you! Right away, he said."

The man glanced back toward the barn, and his eyes got shifty. I looked at the horse and realized he'd probably stolen it before his friends had torched the building. These men were like a crazy mob in the midst of a riot.

"He said he saw you take that horse, sir, and he liked the way you handled it," I said and prayed my guess was right.

The man looked pleased. "Said that, did he?"

I nodded. "The officer said he saw three horses getting away." I pointed in the opposite direction from the way Amalie had run, hoping no one was really hiding out over there. "He saw a secesh loading saddlebags and tying them off on the horses—heavy saddlebags! He thinks they're full of silver! He thinks you can get them back, sir."

The man started to smile. "Good work, boy," he muttered, turning the horse in the direction I'd pointed. He'd forgotten I looked strange.

I turned back toward the trees as the horse cantered away.

Louise stepped out of the shadows, glaring at me. She defiantly brushed the loose hair back out of her eyes. "What will you do with me now?" she practically spat at me.

Still winded from the sprint, I shook my head weakly. "I'm not a soldier," I told her, panting a little. "My name's Alexander Raskin, and I'm a friend of Richeson's."

Her eyes flashed, but she didn't relax. "That could be a lie," she said. "You lied to that Yank about the horses and about getting those clothes from our house."

I straightened up and met her eyes. "I'm sorry about that, but I had to tell him something. I'm not lying about Rich—he told me you two have a hiding place in a hollow of an oak tree over there." I pointed toward the grove behind her. "It's hidden by some branches that hang down low."

She blinked at that detail, then she recovered. "But the Yank was right—you are dressed strangely, and you don't sound like us." She shook her head. "You don't even sound like the Yanks. Who are you? What are you doing here?"

I swallowed. I was going to have to tell her the truth and hope she would believe me. "I told you—I'm Alexander Raskin. And I'm here because Rich told me to find you and make sure you're safe." I took a deep breath. "These clothes— well, they look funny because—because—I'm from a different time."

I saw her eyes widen, and she took a step back from me. I rushed on. "There's no time to explain, because I don't know how long I can stay here. You've got to believe me that I know Rich, and I'm here because he sent me—look, he wrote poetry, and he's got a harmonica." Where was Rich, anyway? He could tell me what to say to her.

I groped for more proof. "He told me how you both were so close and how Amalie and George were close. You two and Jefferson would make up skits for special occasions, and Amalie would play the piano in the parlor at night and your father would sing. George couldn't sing, but he'd recite poetry. Rich can sing—he's got a good baritone."

Louise was smiling now. "You must know him! I don't understand how you come from another time, but you know too much that only Richeson could tell you."

"Louise," I said, then realized that was too forward for 1865 and corrected myself. "Miss Louise—please, tell me where you're going. Rich needs to find you after all this is over. That's why he sent me."

She shook her head, her smile gone now. "I don't know what you should tell my brother. After tonight, I cannot say what will happen. A young soldier, Mr. Andrew Harkens of South Carolina, was staying with us. He had been gravely wounded at Spotsylvania and was sent home on furlough to recover. On his way back to rejoin his regiment at Petersburg, he stopped at our home. But when he heard that Sherman's marauders were headed our way, Mr. Harkens said he would stay with us until they were safely past."

Louise looked at the firelit sky over my shoulder, and her eyes filled with tears. "That can never happen now! But he had made plans with Mr. Baker to take us west if the worst happened. He has friends in Illinois—Confederate sympathizers—in a place called Cairo."

Then she turned back to me. "But I have not thanked you for your courage, Mr. Raskin! You saved me."

"I'm just glad I was here at the right time," I said honestly. "I only did what Rich would have done if he could."

"I left something for him in our special place," she said shyly. "Would you see that he gets it, Mr. Raskin? It is only a small box—it contains a keepsake and a note to tell him we were forced to leave Two Stirrups for Illinois."

I nodded. "I'll see to it." I looked around. There was still no sign of Rich, and that worried me. "We'd better get out of here before that soldier comes back. The Bakers' place is the next farm out, isn't it? Rich told me. Would you like me to go with you?"

She lit up. "Again, I thank you, Mr. Raskin! I am in your debt tonight."

But I walked only a little way with her before we saw figures ahead and heard Amalie's voice: "Louise! Oh, Louise, I thought we'd lost you!"

"Go on," I told her. "I'll make sure Rich knows where you've gone."

She smiled at me and drew herself up and curtsied deeply, holding out one hand. I realized I was supposed to take the hand and kiss it, and I bent over it, gasping from the cold and blushing hot at the same time.

"Thank you, Mr. Raskin," she said as she rose. "You are a true gentleman and a dear friend, wherever you come from." Then she ran ahead to join the others.

I walked back to the cluster of trees, rubbing my arms trying to warm up and searching for Rich. I thought he'd be at their hiding place, but there was no sign of him. I pushed aside the branch, though, and I could see the tin box, shut tight against the rain, waiting for Rich to come for it.

Ignoring the searing cold, I took it down and worked the top loose. There was still enough light from the fires to make out her slanted handwriting.

My dearest brother,

Sherman has come and we have gone with a South Carolina soldier, Mr. Andrew Harkens. Amalie believes he wishes to court her, but I know better! He likes me. He proposes to take us, and the Bakers if they will come, west to friends of his in Illinois, in a place called Cairo. I do not know their names, but surely people will know Mr. Harkens. I will wait for you there. I hope you approve of Mr. Harkens when you meet him. Here is Mother's locket to keep you from loneliness on your journey.

Love,   Louise Chamblee
Two Stirrups   March 29th 1865

I dug in my pockets, wishing I had something like Rich's journal. But all I found was the list of museums and the pencil I'd used to make notes yesterday. I copied Louise's letter, careful to get the lines spaced right and every mark of punctuation correct. If Rich didn't turn up before I went back to my own time, at least I'd have the copy to show him.

Then I carefully wrapped the torn strip of wallpaper around the locket, exactly as I had found it, and put the tin box together as tightly as I could so that one day a construction worker would still find it in the same condition. Exhausted and freezing, I eased myself down on the grass. Why hadn't Rich stayed with me to see Louise for himself and read her letter?

Chapter Sixteen

THE FACE IN
THE LOCKET

"Where have you been?" Dad demanded, furious.

"Out running," I said. I tried to look innocent, even though it was way too late to come back from my run and I wasn't wearing sweats. It had been morning when I awoke, sprawled on the ground under the scrub oaks and pines. I'd felt stiff and tired, even though I'd slept for hours. Rich had never come back. People were arriving for work, and I had to sprint to catch the last shuttle before it stopped running, conjuring up a vivid memory of sprinting toward Louise.

Dad looked from me to the Hambricks. Then he said evenly, "Carleton says you didn't sleep in your bed last night."

Carleton looked up at me with a smug expression, and I wanted to throttle him. His smile turned nervous.

Then Nicole said, "Are you trying to get Alexander in trouble, brat?" She turned to Dad. "He makes up stories all the time, Mr. Raskin. He just wants to be the center of attention. You can't believe anything he says."

Carleton's eyes widened, and his mouth fell open.

"Well, somebody's making up stories, all right," said Mrs. Hambrick.

Nicole tugged on her hair nervously and glared at me.

Carleton's face scrunched up, and I felt miserable. Even if he was a pain sometimes, somebody ought to stick up for him. I figured he was probably mad because I didn't let him run with me the other morning or today. But he was telling the truth.

I made myself say, "I have been out running. But before that I was at Research Triangle Park . . . all night."

Nicole looked surprised. Carleton gave me a wide grin, and I envied him for finding it so easy to forgive.

Dad's round face darkened. "How could you do something so—so—" He was shaking his head in hard little jerks, and his ponytail whipped behind him, "—so irresponsible!"

"I had to help a friend," I said simply.

"A friend?" Dad demanded. "At night? *All* night? And you had to lie to me about it?"

I wouldn't have had to lie if you'd believed me about the ghosts, I wanted to say, but instead I nodded. I needed to figure out how to tell him the truth, but I was too tired.

"You're grounded," Dad said flatly. "Go upstairs and get cleaned up. You're not leaving this house alone."

I nodded again. It was fair, and without Rich, there was nowhere to go anyway.

I dragged myself upstairs and stayed in the shower for a long time. I was hoping to see Rich sitting on my bed, waiting for me when I got out, but he wasn't there. Only Carleton was in the bedroom, hugging his squashed red tyrannosaurus and looking worried.

"Are you mad at me?" he asked as soon as he saw me.

I shook my head and fished in my duffel bag for clean underwear.

"I'm sorry," he whispered into the tyrannosaurus. "I just wanted to go running with you! And you went without me— yesterday and today, both."

"I know. Look, don't worry about it, okay? It doesn't matter."

He watched me dress. "Why did you tell them the truth?" he finally asked. "They'd have believed you more than me."

Maybe. I wasn't too sure about that. Dad hadn't looked ready to believe me—he looked mad enough to lock me inside for life.

"I think they'd have figured it out anyway," I told Carleton as I pulled on my gold "Keep the Past Alive!" T-shirt.

Wind chimes sounded from downstairs and I heard voices. Carleton cocked his head. Then he beamed and jumped up.

"Dr. Seagraves is having lunch with us today," he announced. "She likes my dinosaurs." He ran out with his tyrannosaurus under his arm.

Was it lunchtime already? Had anyone told me Dr. Seagraves was coming to lunch? Probably. Something about her tugged at my memory, but I was too tired to think about it. I lay on my bed hugging Carleton's dumb green stegosaurus, and tried to find the energy to go down and be polite.

"Alexander?" Dad called. "Please come downstairs."

I could hear the tension in his voice. He was still mad, but trying not to show it.

I got to my feet slowly, laid the stegosaurus on the pillow, and went down into the kitchen, avoiding Dad's eyes. Mrs. Hambrick handed me a basket of rolls, and I took it without saying anything. The dining room table was already set, and I put the rolls down next to a salad and went back for the next dish.

Dr. Seagraves held Carleton's tyrannosaurus, pretending to talk to it. She bent down, shaking her head at the red dinosaur until Carleton giggled. Then she straightened, brushed her hair back, and smiled at me. "Hello again, Alexander—historian extraordinaire."

I said, "Hi," and looked away again, embarrassed. She seemed to like me, and I couldn't figure out why.

"I like history, too!" Carleton announced, and she looked at him, distracted by his account of how much fun history museums were.

Relieved, I went back to carrying things. I didn't think I wanted to be any sort of historian. History was more than stories about Odysseus or the War Between the States. I thought of Louise hiding that locket for Rich, and Rich himself, firing and reloading and firing again at Fort Stedman until he ran out of ammunition, then charging with his bayonet. History was real people. I could see the portrait of their mother again, her long black hair and her deep eyes. Even in the picture, those eyes looked full of emotion.

Mrs. Hambrick came into the dining room and told me to sit down. Nicole appeared in time to eat. I tried to ignore the conversation around the table and concentrate on the food.

"How did you enjoy Petersburg?" Dr. Seagraves asked.

I looked up to answer—but nothing came out. I just stared at her.

"Alexander." Dad's voice was strained.

"Is something wrong?" Dr. Seagraves asked. "You've been so quiet today."

"He's grounded," Carleton said.

"Shut up, brat," Nicole muttered. Carleton jumped a little, as if she'd kicked him underneath the table.

"I'm sorry," I said at last, confused at my reaction. "Petersburg was great." I scooped some salad onto my plate and passed the bowl to Nicole.

I picked up my fork, but didn't take a bite. I stared again at Dr. Seagraves. There was something important about her—something about her face. But what was it?

Then I realized everyone was looking at me staring at her, and I flushed.

"I—I'm sorry," I stammered. "Really. It's just—I've seen you somewhere before."

"Like at the university?" Nicole asked, rolling her eyes. "Like over here for supper the other night?"

Dr. Seagraves looked at me, her black eyes grave and sympathetic, and I set the fork down suddenly. Dr. Seagraves, and the locket, and Louise's message for Rich . . .

"No," I said, more slowly. "Not in person—I meant a picture of you. I've seen a picture since I met you at the university."

Why had it taken me so long? I should have recognized those eyes and that hair when she was talking to Carleton. She reached up one hand nervously to brush it back from her face, and I could see Louise brushing the loose hair out of her eyes last night and Rich brushing his shorter hair back the same way. Dr. Seagraves' thick black hair was like theirs, and like the woman's in the locket miniature. And her eyes were the familiar deep black eyes I'd seen so often in Rich's face. But I didn't know how to tell her what I knew.

"Your family," I tried to explain. "You were trying to trace your family, and you couldn't find out who your great-great—" I shook my head. "I'm not sure how many greats—grandmother was. But you knew she came from around here, right?"

"She came from North Carolina," Dr. Seagraves said slowly, looking confused.

"Alexander, that's enough," Dad said, his eyebrows nearly meeting in the middle of his forehead.

"I think we should listen," Mrs. Hambrick interjected. "He's been—very caught up in history since he got here." She studied me. "Go on, Alexander."

I took a deep breath. "You said she came out of North Carolina to Missouri, but you didn't know her maiden name, and you couldn't trace your family back any further. Well, I know who she was."

Dr. Seagraves stiffened in her chair, her hand clenching the edge of the table.

Dad said, "Alexander?"

"Wait!" Mrs. Hambrick reached across the corner of the table and laid one hand on my father's arm. "Let him finish, Bill."

I swallowed. "Her name was Louise Chamblee," I told Dr. Seagraves. "You can see a picture of her mother in a locket at the museum we went to on Tuesday. That picture looks so much like you—it could *be* you! I mean that."

Dad let his breath out. "Alexander—an old picture could look like anyone."

I shook my head. "It's not just the picture." I turned back to Dr. Seagraves as another piece of the puzzle fell into place. That clinched it. "You said her husband was named Andrew Harkens, didn't you? But you couldn't find any Andrew Harkens in North Carolina who went to Missouri?"

She nodded, surprised. "How did you remember all that?"

I couldn't understand why I hadn't remembered it sooner. "Well, you couldn't find him in North Carolina, because his family lived in South Carolina. He was on his way back to his regiment at Petersburg when Sherman's raiders came through, and he saved Louise and her sister Amalie."

The room was silent. Now I realized why I had come to Durham, and why I was the right out-of-timer for Rich. Richeson, Louise, Dr. Seagraves—they all had pieces of a puzzle, but they needed me to bring them together so they could find the answers they needed.

"She wrote a letter telling her . . . brother where they were going," I said, my voice cracking at the word *brother*. "It was wrapped around the locket. It's all messed up, but they have it at the museum, too."

"He's right about the picture and the name Chamblee," Nicole said, backing me up unexpectedly. "But the woman at the museum said the note was illegible. How did you find out it said all that, Alexander?"

"I don't understand at all," said Dr. Seagraves, her black eyes troubled. "How could you learn all this? And why would you try to find out about my family?"

I shook my head, helplessly. "I didn't know I was—until now. I found this out for someone else, someone who knew Louise Chamblee and that she disappeared in the spring of 1865. Last night I found out about Andrew Harkens, and it wasn't until I really looked at you today that I realized what was so familiar about—" I started to say Rich and Louise but stopped myself, "—about the portrait in the locket."

"What happened last night?" Dr. Seagraves asked.

At the same time, Dad asked, "Who was this someone else? Was that who you were with last night?"

I didn't know how else to answer, except with the truth. "His name is Richeson Chamblee."

"The family is still here?" Dr. Seagraves asked, her eyes lighting up.

"He's the friend!" Dad exclaimed. "What were the two of you doing at Research Triangle Park in the middle of the night?"

I had to shake my head at Dr. Seagraves. "I don't think any of the family is left around here."

"Then—" Dad started. Mrs. Hambrick reached out to him again, and he stopped. But he looked confused—and somehow hurt.

I swallowed. "Richeson Chamblee was a Confederate soldier who died at Fort Stedman. He wanted to know what happened to his sister. Last night was the anniversary of Sherman's raid on the Chamblees' farm. Their house was near where the computer company is now, in Research Triangle Park. So I went there, and I found Louise, and she told me she was leaving with Andrew Harkens. He was taking her and her sister Amalie to Cairo in Illinois—he had friends there."

Nobody said anything.

"They were ghosts," I said in a small voice, feeling sick. I knew no one would believe me.

Dad jerked away from Mrs. Hambrick and stood up so hard the dining room chair rocked on its legs. "Alexander!" he practically shouted.

Dr. Seagraves just sat there looking at me.

"Ghosts?" asked Carleton.

Nicole smiled slowly. "So that's what the cold was."

Mrs. Hambrick glanced at her and then at my dad, but she spoke to me. "Don't look so stricken, Alexander. You seem to have taken this in stride up to now. Have you seen ghosts before?"

I couldn't tell if she was making fun of me or not. She didn't seem to be, but I didn't trust her. I nodded.

"Stop it, Alexander," Dad said, his voice breaking. "Paige—I can't believe you're encouraging him!"

She sighed, but she didn't get angry. "I love the precision of statistics," she said thoughtfully. "I like wind chimes for the precise musical notes they ring out."

"The wind chimes made a lot of noise this week," Carleton interrupted. "Was that the ghost?" I nodded again.

Mrs. Hambrick didn't look surprised. "Based on the wind and the experience of listening to them over time, I can sometimes predict which chime will sound. But they've been different this week." She looked at my father. "I love the way mathematical probability tells me what I *can* predict, but I think it's just as important that it shows me there are unexpected insights that *can't* be predicted."

Nicole suddenly interrupted. "Daddy understood that, didn't he? That's why he got you all those wind chimes?"

Mrs. Hambrick smiled in agreement. "If Alexander says a ghost told him about Louise Chamblee, then I'm prepared to believe him, even if I've never seen a ghost myself."

I looked at Mrs. Hambrick, stunned. It was as if I'd never seen her before. I wasn't seeing the woman Nicole had teased me about hating, or the math whiz who thought like one of Dad's computers. She had a whole deeper level I never realized existed. I wondered if she'd surprised Dad, too.

Dr. Seagraves nodded once, decisively. "I don't know what to believe, but I understand about unexpected insights. That happens in historical work all the time, when you think you know where your research is taking you, and then you look at the facts in a new arrangement and you realize they mean something entirely different."

She turned to me. "Alexander, I want to see this locket—and the note."

Chapter Seventeen

TEAMWORK

At first I didn't think Dad was going to come with us, but then he asked Mrs. Hambrick if she would ride to the museum with Dr. Seagraves. "We'll meet you there," he told them. "I need to talk to Alexander alone."

I felt my insides tighten. He still didn't believe me.

I climbed into the front passenger seat of Mrs. Hambrick's van, not looking at her or Dr. Seagraves in the driveway behind me. Dad waved briefly at them, fumbled with the unfamiliar controls, then fired up the engine.

We were barely out of the driveway when he started in on me, but it wasn't what I had expected. "Out all night trying to track down ghosts?" he practically shouted. "What if something had happened to you?"

"Nothing happened," I said, glad I hadn't mentioned the guards or the fact that I was real enough in the ghosts' time to risk getting hit by a Yankee bullet at the farm.

"Besides—you never believed me." My anger flared. "And since we got here, you've been so busy with Mrs. Hambrick, I didn't think I mattered. You never care what I want, about going back to Indiana. I bet you got that job here, didn't you?"

He turned the corner, heading toward downtown. "Yes. They offered me the job."

I twisted the lariat tighter around my wrist. "And you took it, right?"

Dad didn't say anything for a minute. Then he asked, "You know how I've always been so big on teamwork? Well, it's not a big thing in programming, actually. We each work in our own special niche." I thought of the way Rich had described all those little rooms, with people shut inside staring at lighted windows, all alone. Dad went on, "Teamwork is something your mother taught me."

My jaw dropped. He never had anything good to say about Mom.

"But you two were the team," he said. "I always felt like I was on the outside looking in. When she left, I wanted us to be a team—you and me. I wanted to be there for you—remember how I used to go out with a stopwatch and time you when you were getting ready to try out for the track team?"

That startled me. I suddenly remembered Dad huddled in a bright green, hooded raincoat, water dripping into his eyes as he cupped one hand over the stopwatch and peered at the time. When I beat my own record that rainy day, he laughed and hugged me.

He was right that I knew what teamwork meant. You run alone in track, but at a meet it's the sum of the individual scores that counts. I cheered Gary and the other guys, and I could hear them cheering when I ran.

"You always tried to be there for me, too," Dad was saying. "But when this happened, you couldn't tell me."

"Dad—I tried to tell you—a long time ago," I protested, "when I saw those ghosts back home, the soldiers in armor."

The light turned red, and he slowed the van to a halt. "De Soto's men," he said. "I remember."

"You didn't believe me when I said they were ghosts— only Mom did." I felt angry again.

He was silent as the light changed and he drove through the intersection. "Your mother's gone, Alexander."

"She's coming back!" I practically screamed at him. "I made a vow that I'd wait for her!"

He slammed on the brakes and skidded to the side of the street. He threw the gearshift into Park and put his hands over his face. I didn't realize he was crying until he looked up. "Oh, Alexander," he said softly, "she's not, no matter what you vowed. You can't make her come back just because you want her to, any more than I could. Your mother gets— intense about things. She keeps trying to find out why she

198

was put here on earth, and when she thinks something's the reason, whatever that something is matters to her more than anything else. But it only lasts for a little while, and then she decides there has to be a more important cause, and she starts looking for it."

"No," I said. I didn't want to hear it, like I hadn't wanted to hear it when Dad told me he'd gotten a divorce. So what if Mom got intense about things?

Then I remembered the recorder. Once she had told me that she was here to make beautiful music. But she hadn't played it for months before she left. Maybe it was just one more thing she got bored with and abandoned.

"She was really intense about having a family," Dad said, "and she cared so much about you that she was sure you were her reason for being. She loved you very much, Alexander. She still does, I'm sure. But that won't bring her back."

I tried to shake my head. What about her flowers? I wanted to ask. But I knew the answer. The garden had almost died before she left. Dad helped me bring it back. The roses—the bushes I'd tended for her—she hadn't planted them. Dad was the one who dug the holes and heaved the bundles of wooden branches with their burlap-wrapped root balls into the dirt. Dad had planted them for me, because I'd been upset that the garden was dying.

"I know how much you love her," he said. And I suddenly wondered—how much *did* I love her? As much as Rich loved his dead mother and his lost sister? Or as much as Carleton and Nicole loved their dead father? How much did I love the father who'd stayed by me?

Dad paused, squeezing the steering wheel and staring through the windshield. "I love Paige and I want to marry her," he said quietly. "I want to take the job and move here and make Paige and her kids part of our team. But you're the most important person in my life, Alexander. If you won't— if you can't—if you totally hate the idea—then you and I will go back to Indiana."

I stared out my window. My reflection had turned blurry, as if something was wrong with my eyes. Dad hadn't left me. If I was put on this earth to help the people I cared about, I couldn't spend all my life caring most for someone who had left. I turned in the seat, leaned against Dad's shoulder, and cried.

I felt his arms close around me.

"Remember how hard you worked to plant those rose bushes?" I asked some time later. Dad kept his hold on me.

I could feel his chest heave in a sigh. "Unfortunately, I do," he said.

"Well, how'd you like to dig them up and move them to North Carolina?" I asked, ignoring the wrench of pain at what a final decision that would be. But it was the right decision, no matter how much it hurt. "I bet Carleton would love to help us dig in the dirt."

Dad leaned back so he could look at me. "I bet he would."
He hugged me tighter. "Thank you, Alexander."

I hugged him back and whispered, "I love you, too."

He smiled, turning the van back into traffic. As we drove
to the museum, I told him the whole story of stumbling onto
Rich and finding Louise.

———〜〜〜———

Chapter Eighteen

LOUISE

When we pulled up at the museum, Dr. Seagraves and Mrs. Hambrick were standing on the sidewalk outside the porch. And they weren't alone—Nicole and Carleton had come along.

Carleton ran up to me. "We were waiting for you."

I smiled. "I'm glad you did." I turned to the others and took a deep breath. "Come on."

When I opened the screen door into the humid hallway, Ms. Edwards looked up. She seemed surprised to see such a large group, then she recognized me and stood up. "Alexander! Welcome back."

"Hi," I told her. "This is my dad, and this is Mrs. Hambrick, Carleton and Nicole's mom. And this is Dr. Seagraves from Duke. I brought her to see the portrait in the locket."

I didn't realize how much I'd been hoping Rich would be here until I turned the corner and felt the same warm air as in the front hall. I hadn't seen him since last night. But all I smelled was the mustiness of old things, with a hint of cedar. No oranges.

"See?" Nicole said. "The name's Chamblee, and the portrait looks just like you, the way Alexander said."

"The resemblance is remarkable," said Ms. Edwards, looking slowly from the miniature to Dr. Seagraves.

The professor just stood there, studying the image of a woman who had died in 1859—a face that could have been her reflection in a mirror except for her clothes and the way she wore her hair.

"Look at those eyes," Mrs. Hambrick said. "They're exactly like yours."

After holding Louise's note in my hands last night, I wanted one last look at the fragments that had been recovered. As soon as I eased the door into the back room open a crack, the smell of oranges and the cold air hit me.

Rich stood beside the table where the torn strip of wallpaper still lay between the glass plates. He didn't look up as I shut the door and hurried to him.

"I found her," I told him. "I found out what happened! She was all right, Rich!"

He slowly raised his head, his eyes black holes of misery. One fist gripped his musket. "I couldn't help her. I wish I'd never left Two Stirrups for the Army. And I wish I'd never tried to go back. I'm sorry I ever dragged you into this."

"But it worked out, Rich—I got rid of the Yankee, and I took her to where Amalie was waiting for her. First I had to get her to trust me—I even had to tell her I was from a different time, but she believed me because I convinced her I knew you and that you'd sent me."

He reached through the glass plates, his hands opening and closing helplessly through the piece of wallpaper. "Don't you understand, Alexander? I can accept the fact that I died for my country—but I cannot accept the fate that befell my family afterward! Going back to Two Stirrups last night showed me that it was all for nothing. I couldn't save Louise or Amalie."

"That's not true! You couldn't save Louise then—you were already a ghost! But you held Fort Stedman long enough to cover the retreat, and that saved a lot of lives. That counted for something! And your friend Noah was right—while you were standing fast at Fort Stedman, someone else was there for Louise and Amalie."

"You were, but what happened to them had already happened. You can't change history," he said bitterly.

"Not me," I told him, "a man from South Carolina named Andrew Harkens. He'd been wounded at Spotsylvania and sent home on furlough, but he decided he was going to make a last stand against the Yankees at Petersburg. He passed through Wake County on his way to his regiment, and he stayed at Two Stirrups. And when your sisters learned that Sherman's men were on the way, he stayed to protect them.

After the soldiers burned your farm, the three of them left together, because everything was falling apart."

Rich stared at me. "How could you know?"

"I know it because Louise told me, and because I saw him take Louise and Amalie to the Bakers'. And you can believe it because Louise wrote it down for you."

I unfolded the piece of paper I'd copied her note onto and spread it out next to the faded, bleached piece of wallpaper for Rich to read.

After he finished, Rich looked up, the lines in his face relaxing. "She waited for me," he said.

I nodded. "And Mr. Harkens married her. I'm sure Louise knew you would have approved if you had been able to meet him."

Rich looked puzzled. "Louise couldn't have told you about her marriage."

"After they got married and realized you weren't coming, they went to Missouri," I went on, adding Dr. Seagraves' story to what Louise had told me. "Louise had a daughter who grew up and had children. Louise's line didn't die out, Rich."

"But how do you *know*?" he insisted.

"Because I met—" I began, when the door opened behind me.

"It's in here," Ms. Edwards was saying. "Don't mind the cold. For some reason this room has been very chilly lately." Then she saw me. "Alexander? What are you doing?"

"I just wanted another look at the note, Ms. Edwards," I said quickly, reaching for my sheet of paper.

"And what's that?" She looked at it in surprise. "Is this supposed to be the rest of the note?" Ms. Edwards pulled it toward her before I had time to shove it into my pocket.

She looked up, smiling. "Did you make this up? It's quite good."

"Actually, Alexander is very accurate about historical things, Ms. Edwards," said Mrs. Hambrick. She looked back and forth from the fragments to my copy of Louise's letter. "Look at the spacing of the words—you can see the salutation, and part of 'Sherman.' The other fragments fit the words you can read."

Dr. Seagraves bent forward to see it, and Rich cried out, "Louise?"

Dr. Seagraves looked around, as if she'd felt something, and I suddenly wondered if she could hear him, or at least a distant whisper of his voice. "Is there a cold draft in here?" she asked.

"That's Alexander's ghost," said Carleton. "Brrrrrr!"

"The cold," Nicole explained.

"I remember," Mrs. Hambrick said, looking thoughtfully at me.

"Louise was your—what?—great-grandmother, Dr. Seagraves?" I asked. "Is that right?"

"Apparently," Dr. Seagraves said. "What was her brother's name? Richeson?"

"Richeson Francis Chamblee," I told her, and she looked up in surprise. "For Francis Scott Key," I added, but she still looked amazed.

"I'd say that clinches it," said Mrs. Hambrick. "I don't think you've ever heard Dr. Seagraves' full name, Alexander."

Dr. Seagraves turned her black eyes on me. "My first name is Louise," she said, "and my middle name is Frances. My grandmother was named Frances Louise. The names have been passed on."

Rich had tears in his eyes. "Louise named her baby after me."

"I don't know how to begin to thank you, Alexander," Dr. Seagraves said. "You found my great-grandmother for me."

"I'm not sure how you came up with this, Alexander, but may I make a copy to keep?" asked Ms. Edwards. "I know there's no historical proof that the note actually said anything like this . . ." Her voice trailed off.

"But sometimes you just know something is true without having any proof," Mrs. Hambrick finished for her.

Ms. Edwards looked at Dr. Seagraves. "Well, your resemblance to the portrait is certainly proof that there's something to this story!"

"Could you make me a copy also?" asked Dr. Seagraves.

As they walked to a copier machine in the far corner, Rich said quietly, "Thank you, Alexander. Thank you for letting me see Louise's great-granddaughter. Waiting all these years, not knowing—standing fast at Fort Stedman—it *was* all worth it."

I looked across at Mrs. Hambrick, a little ways behind Dr. Seagraves at the copier. Dad was standing next to her, holding her hand and smiling. Rich had been right—Mom hadn't left because of me. She'd left because of her own problems. I had to accept that I couldn't change that. All I could do was love her anyway and get on with my life. "You're welcome," I told Rich and meant it. "Helping you was worth it for me, too."

Carleton came up to me. "Are you talking to your ghost? Is he haunting you now?"

I smiled at Rich over Carleton's head. "I don't think he's going to haunt anybody anymore," I said to Carleton. "I tell you what—how would you like to help me plant rose bushes in your yard? You'd get to dig up lots of dirt."

Carleton beamed. "I can dig a trench!" Then he asked, "Will there be more ghosts in the yard?"

I grinned. "You never can tell."

Carleton ran over to tell his mother about the rose bushes.

When I looked up, Rich was gone.

"Good-bye, Richeson Francis Chamblee," I whispered. "Trust me. You stood fast—and it counted for a lot."

Then I realized that Mrs. Hambrick and my dad were beside me, still holding hands. "Thank you, Alexander," she said, very softly.

"Oh, great," I heard Nicole sighing behind her. "Now I get stuck with two kid brothers." But she sounded almost pleased at the idea.

Dad pointed to my "Keep the Past Alive!" shirt. "I think we should get a set," he said, "for the whole family."

It sounded strange—the whole family. Was I ready for that? I took my copy of Louise's letter back from Ms. Edwards and folded it carefully. I wanted to keep it so that I could always remember the girl who wrote those words and the boy she'd left them for—a family that wanted to hang on to each other, no matter what. But I knew now the past was a pattern that had already grown and flowered. What mattered was the way I planted and tended the patterns that would shape my future. I glanced down at the remnants of Louise's note under the glass, then up at Dad and Mrs. Hambrick, still standing close to each other. I was finally ready to start growing whatever new patterns the future had in store for me.

Author's Note

The attack on Fort Stedman was a real battle in the nine-month siege of Petersburg that ended the Civil War or, as many Southerners call it, the War Between the States. Richeson Francis Chamblee is a fictional character, similar to many underage Southern teens who volunteered in the last desperate months of the war.

In an effort to wear down General Lee's Army of Northern Virginia, General Grant's Union Army assaulted the city of Petersburg in the summer of 1864. Confederate President Jefferson Davis refused to leave his capital in Richmond, so Lee had no choice but to defend Petersburg in order to protect the railroad to Richmond. He had his soldiers dig trenches and construct earthworks to create a siege line defending the city. The Union Army responded with a series of attacks to the southwest, slowly encircling Petersburg and cutting the Southern railroads leading up to the city, thereby gradually starving the Southern troops and the people of Petersburg. By the spring of 1865, casualties from battle, starvation, and disease had taken such a toll that General Lee informed President Davis the Army would have to retreat.

In March 1865, General Gordon came up with a daring alternative. Gordon's men defended a part of the Southern line called Colquitt's Salient, which was very close to the Northern line. Like the Confederate Army, the Union soldiers had dug trenches and built earthen forts all along their line. But General Gordon's soldiers were so close to one fort, Fort Stedman, that he thought his men could move forward quietly in the night, launch a surprise attack, and seize the fort. Once done, Gordon believed he had a chance to attack other parts of the Union line from the rear, capture supplies, and perhaps even break the siege.

Gordon's plan worked, and his troops captured Fort Stedman just before dawn on March 25, 1865. But after that, things didn't go as planned. Northern soldiers at the other forts heard the fighting at Fort Stedman and sent thousands of reinforcements. When Gordon's men tried to continue their attack, they were overwhelmed by the Northern counterattack and almost captured. General Gordon managed to get some of his men back to Colquitt's Salient because a regiment of North Carolina infantry held Fort Stedman against the Union counterattack until the very end. In that morning's fighting alone, the two armies combined suffered more than five thousand casualties.

After the failure to hold Fort Stedman and break the Union line, General Lee pulled his army out and let Petersburg fall to the Northern Army. General Grant pursued him to Appomattox, where Lee surrendered the remains of the Army of Northern Virginia, effectively ending the war.

Some readers may find it difficult to understand how someone like Richeson, a teenager from a family that didn't even own slaves, could feel so strongly about fighting for the Confederacy. Although ending slavery was a major outcome of the War, it is a great simplification to say that the War was fought over slavery. The causes of the War were many and complex, involving political and economic concerns. For example, the federal government's primary income was from tariffs on imported goods. A greater Northern population represented more votes in Congress, and tariffs controlling international trade with Europe were enacted so as to protect growing Northern industry at the expense of the agrarian South.

The eleven Southern states that eventually seceded also maintained that the federal government was taking too much authority upon itself. They believed that individual states should determine policy for their citizens. They based this belief, which they called States' Rights, on the principles of the Founding Fathers of the United States, who united equal and sovereign states for their mutual protection and benefit. One of the rights some Southerners wanted upheld was certainly the right to own slaves, but even Southerners who found the idea of slavery repugnant supported States'

Rights on issues such as tariffs, free trade, access to railroads, Atlantic shipping, and many others. Of the total number of Southern soldiers fighting in the War, fewer than one in nine came from a slave-owning household—fewer than one in three Southern households owned even a single slave. By the end of the War, one of every two male Southerners old enough to fight had been either killed or maimed—citizens don't make that level of sacrifice solely to allow wealthy plantation owners to profit from their slaves' labor.

Despite the willingness of Southern citizens to fight for their beliefs, the larger Union Armies consistently outnumbered the Confederate troops they faced. With its densely populated industrial cities, the Northern government had a larger population base to draw on and used conscription to draft laborers and newly arrived immigrants. The Union Army expected an easy victory, but early Confederate successes discouraged the North and brought favorable reaction from Europe. In order to inspire the North, and to prevent potential European intervention, President Lincoln used the abolition of slavery as a rallying cry. He raised this issue for the first time only at Gettysburg in 1863.

By 1864, Union generals revised their war plans. Knowing the large difference in population, General Grant developed a strategy of attrition: he would repeatedly attack General Lee's Army of Northern Virginia, accepting huge, but replaceable, losses among his own soldiers in order to achieve smaller, but irreplaceable, losses in the Southern Army.

General Sherman took Grant's plan one step further. Unlike Union troops, who were issued uniforms and supplies, Southern soldiers wore uniforms made by their mothers or wives, and were supplied largely from home, from funds raised by donations, and from farms they passed. Therefore, General Sherman proposed destroying the supply base for the Southern troops by destroying their farms and homes. Known as Sherman's March, this attack on civilians first swept through Georgia, then up into South Carolina and North Carolina. General Sheridan did the same in the Shenandoah Valley of Virginia. The generals vowed to leave behind them nothing but barren land. Sheridan even boasted that a crow flying over the Shenandoah "would have to bring his own provender."

Northern soldiers burned farmhouses, barns, and crops, and killed or stole all livestock. To prevent any future fundraising for the Confederacy, they seized heirlooms and valuables, killing family members or slaves who resisted. They tore up the railroads to destroy transportation in the South. After pulling up the iron railroad tracks, the soldiers heated them in fires and twisted the metal around fruit trees, killing the trees and destroying the track.

Many of the Northern soldiers were brutal, and it's all too easy to think of them as villains for attacking civilians so ruthlessly. However, it might be more realistic to see the soldiers involved as men who were given shameful orders. Perhaps they could not justify the orders morally, and therefore degenerated into a mob mentality so they would not have to face up to their actions. Not since the Roman destruction of Carthage and Judea had any organized national army destroyed civilian homes and property like Sherman's and Sheridan's men. Confronted with this unmilitary invasion, it's easy to see how teenagers like Richeson volunteered near the end of the War, determined to protect their families and homes.

I would like to thank my critique group in Bloomington, Indiana, for their patient help and encouragement through numerous critical readings of this book. I would especially like to thank my editor, Christy Ottaviano, for proposing I write a new War Between the States ghost story, for giving me the confidence to experiment with a new voice in this book, and for offering kind but firm guidance in focusing Alexander's story.

Finally, I would like to thank my husband, Lieutenant Colonel Arthur B. Alphin (Ret.), for taking time off from his work to give me a military tour of the National Battlefield Park at Petersburg, for providing me with photographs of the battlefield and of Confederate soldiers, and for letting me practice loading and firing his antique musket. I am grateful for his insightful and technical readings of many versions of this manuscript. Beyond his tangible help on this book, I appreciate his faithful support of my writing through the years and his unyielding determination to stand fast against injustice. He is an enduring inspiration to me.

Boulder City Library
701 Adams Boulevard
Boulder City, NV 89005

DISCARD

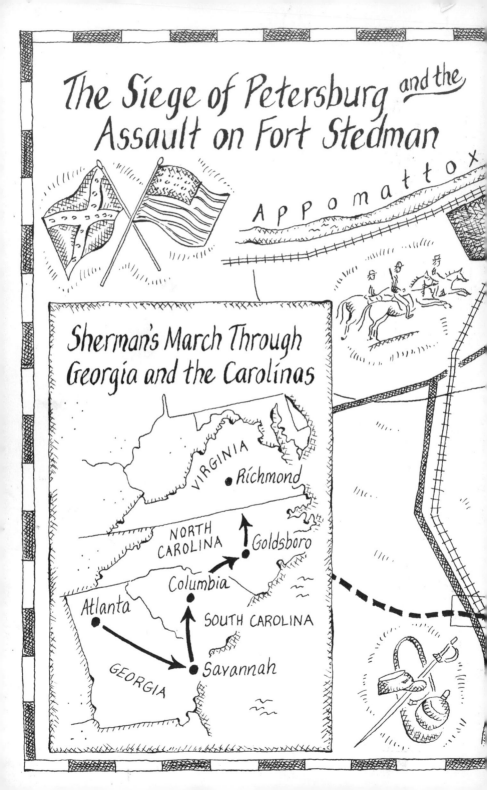